T0405882

Beyond All
Reasonable Doubt,
JESUS IS ALIVE!

Beyond All
Reasonable Doubt,
JESUS IS ALIVE!

Stories

Melissa Lozada-Oliva

ASTRA HOUSE
New York

For information about permission to reproduce selections from this book, please
contact permissions@astrahouse.com.

Astra House
A Division of Astra Publishing House
astrahouse.com
Printed in the United States of America

Two of the stories were previously published:

"Pool House" was published through Audible in 2020 in a different version.

"Something Loving: appeared in Cake Zine's *Tough Cookie* in 2023
as "First Fridays."

Library of Congress Cataloging-in-Publication Data

Names: Lozada-Oliva, Melissa author
Title: Beyond all reasonable doubt, Jesus is alive! : stories / Melissa Lozada-Oliva.
Description: First edition. | New York : Astra House, 2025. | Summary:
"A spiky and surprising short story collection about women and their
demons: jealous men, predatory teachers, monsters, fame, inherited
trauma, and their own personal BS"— Provided by publisher.
Identifiers: LCCN 2025011742 | ISBN 9781662601828 hardcover |
ISBN 9781662601835 epub
Subjects: LCGFT: Short stories
Classification: LCC PS3612.O958 B49 2025 | DDC 813/.6—dc23/eng/20250501
LC record available at https://lccn.loc.gov/2025011742

ISBN: 9781662601828

First edition
10 9 8 7 6 5 4 3 2 1

Design by Alissa Theodor
The text is set in Warnock Pro Light.
The titles are set in Averia Serif Libre.

For my friends, alive and not

God made everything out of nothing. But the nothingness shows through.

—Paul Valéry

Contents

Beyond All
Reasonable Doubt,
JESUS IS ALIVE!

Beyond All Reasonable Doubt, Jesus Is Alive!

We found out our third-grade teacher, Mr. Greco, was a VIP member of a child porn ring the day you were trying on wedding dresses. The first rushes of love for us came from watching Mr. Greco hang sideways from a pole on the playground during recess. He had been twenty-three then and had a stocky gymnast's body. Of course you fall in love with someone like that: when they're making it look like gravity doesn't apply to them. I was scrolling through my phone when I saw the article.

"What?" you said, turning around. A wooden clip held the back of your dress together.

"They found him upstate on the run, I guess." I said it like I was telling you about something else that was inconsequential, a new disease carried by mosquitos across the ocean.

"Jesus," you said, turning back around and facing the mirror. "Weren't you just there?" You're curvier than I am. I was always the skinny, tall one with no tits, long spaghetti limbs dangling in front of me. I've always been jealous of your milkmaid body, all the estrogen pumping through it.

"That one is nice," I told you. "The neckline is good." You looked yourself up and down like you always do, unaffected by the vessel assigned to you, like you were looking up from knitting to watch a reality TV show kept on in the background.

"Yeah? I guess I'll take it. Let's just do that. I'm fucking tired of being here." You paid for the dress with a swipe of your credit card. You're a coffee trainer and you just got promoted. It's a job that's perfect for you because it came out of necessity. You love the rhythm of it: the popping into shops and fixing espresso machines, teaching baristas how to heat up milk without creating a pig-slaughtering noise. You make them feel comfortable even though they're all hungover idiots. You're patient with them. You've told me that there is no ethical way to drink coffee—it's a blood bean, you called it—but you could get as close as possible. Your dream is to be an importer, because then you could travel. I can picture you at a port somewhere in Colombia, this Korean girl with Spanish better than mine, learning something about the history that I was too lazy or anxious to. We've been friends for a little more than two decades, which means that we will be friends forever, unless one of us does something unspeakable, but even then there would be forgiveness. If I ever fucked your husband, you would laugh. If you ever killed anybody I loved, I knew it would be for a good reason and I'd help you bury the body. It isn't manic, what is between us. We ate gentrification taco bowls close to Delancey, and you paid for my meal. I made a little big deal about it for show, like, *Oh, I couldn't possibly, but actually, please.*

"So, what happened?"

"Uh, it's pretty bad."

"Now I need to know everything."

"It was nobody under thirteen."

"What a saint."

"I mean, it's still *bad.*"

"What would he do to them?" I winced over what I was about to say, but it was almost in the same way that I sometimes only wash my hands in a public bathroom if somebody else is there. The public performance of courtesy.

"A lot of it was just, like, sharing videos. He was an access point, I guess? But also he would drug these teens that he would babysit and take off their clothes and just, like, lie next to them? And take videos of that."

"Who babysits teens?"

"I don't know. When you're thirteen, you're a teenager, right?"

"When you're thirteen, you're a child." You sipped the last of your horchata and chewed thoughtfully on the bamboo straw. You looked at me and lifted your eyebrows.

"What?" I said. "I don't think he ever did."

"How would we know? It was so long ago. Do you think you can trust your memories?"

"He was just so nice to my mom. And to me."

"He was probably grooming you. Probably grooming the both of us. My God."

"Yeah." I dipped a crooked chip into guac that looked like soft-serve ice cream, a perfectly swirled green turd. It needed more salt. "Fucked up."

"What would Nick say about this?" you asked, examining your freshly done nails: pink and glowing half-moons with white lightning bolts delicately drawn on each one.

"I actually don't think he had him."

"Oh, right."

"But probably something earnest."

"Yeah, he'd be like, 'Let's check in on everybody's capacity right now.'"

"And then he'd meaningfully hold our hands and look us in the eye, and we wouldn't be able to stop laughing."

"He'd probably cry."

"Fucking moron."

"So stupid."

"Miss him."

"Me too." You stacked our aluminum take-out trays on top of each other in an elegant tower.

"You're definitely not bringing a plus-one to the wedding?"

"You can give that spot up, it's fine."

"You doing okay?"

"Yeah, why?"

"I don't know, without Vern?"

"Sure, I feel good."

"Where are you staying?"

"Friend's couch."

"Okay." I could tell you didn't want to push. You knew how I felt when people treated me like I was a kid. "Well, just let me know if you need anything." You jangled your car keys and stood up, and I with you, our chairs creaking together.

Here's the thing, Laura. I'd seen Mr. Greco just weeks before, when I was cat sitting upstate in Ithaca for my old professor, but I haven't told you about it yet. I had just ended my one-year tryst with Vern during an argument about the soap dispenser. I started laughing uncontrollably, and he just was getting madder and madder. I thought he was going to punch a wall, and I had tears streaming down my face, just laughing. "What the hell is wrong with you, Andy?" he screamed at me. I told him that we had to break up and I would move out. I texted you and said I would no longer need a plus-one to your wedding, to which you responded with *That's fine, Kevin's cousin wanted to bring a date.* I don't think you ever liked Vern.

My professor told me to stop at a pie shop called Julie's because it had good pie and a nice view of the mountains, so I did. I had most of my things in my car and had been sleeping in it for a week. I hadn't told you that either, but I felt like maybe you knew, and maybe that's why you paid for my taco bowl, and also because you sniffed my armpit and said, "Did you know that there's no proof that aluminum actually gives you breast cancer?" You fucking bitch. I ordered an apple crumble pie that went by the name of Lets-Have-A-Crumble and then remembered that, actually, I hate pie and the way it can taste like a nursing home at noon. So I walked to the trash can with most of my Lets-Have-A-Crumble still on its paper plate, and there was Mr. Greco, right next to the trash can, sitting on a picnic bench. He was wearing a faded green shirt that I could see his pecs through and white linen pants. There was a black backpack by his fleshy feet, which were in a pair of blue rubber sandals. He was sipping from a Diet Coke and looked exactly the same, just a little more weathered, like a nicely worn boot.

"Mr. Greco!" He was staring off into the mountains. It really was a nice view. I couldn't tell if he was pretending not to hear me. I was only feet away. If I fell a certain way, I would've landed right in his lap. I tried again. A bee landed on a gooey piece of apple, then flew away.

"Mr. Greco." And then it was like he turned on, like my saying his name again had wound him up. He smiled at me with those cheeks I remembered, deep dimples on either side of his mouth.

"Andy?" he said. "Wow! It's been years. Holy shit!" He slapped his leg and shook his head, the lines around his eyes bunching up in a way that is always attractive in men and never in women. It was weird to hear him swear. I tossed the pie into the trash can and heard it land on the bottom. Sweet, unfinished trash. An old man with a Band-Aid on his face took a seat at the end of the table with a piece of raspberry pie. His hands shook as he lifted the plastic fork holding the bloody morsel to his chapped lips.

"How the hell are ya? Didn't like the pie?"

"I don't really like sweets."

"I'm jealous. I've got such a sweet tooth." He smiled again. "Sometimes it gets me in trouble." He scratched at his beard.

"Yeah, I'm kind of a freak like that!" I let out one of my laughs that you say sounds like a laugh lost its batteries.

"What are you doing out here, Andy?"

"Oh, I'm cat sitting in Ithaca."

"Wonderful!" he said, sipping from his Diet Coke. "I'm headed there too."

"You are?" Flies circled around the trash can. I swatted one away.

"Yup. Catching the bus in an hour."

"I could just give you a ride." I know.

"No, no, please, that would be really embarrassing for me."

"It's no problem for me at all." I'm really insane.

"I couldn't put you out like that. I really appreciate it, but it's really okay."

"Just chip in for some gas," I said. "I insist." You're gonna hate me by the end of this.

In the car, I was aware of all my immaturities: the faded, molding coffee in the Dunkin' Donuts cup from two weeks ago in the cupholder. The empty bag of Zapp's chips in the other cupholder. The records and boxes of books and dance costumes in the back seat. All the cartoon figurines I'd collected through the years that bounced and jiggled while the car moved forward.

"Sorry about the mess."

"Please," he said to me, "I'm just grateful for the ride." He clicked in his seat belt.

"Here"—I handed him my phone—"type the address in my phone."

"Doesn't look like you have service right now."

"Really? Shit. Well, um, let's just wait for it to come back, and maybe in the meantime, I'll just drive down I-81."

"That sounds fine to me," he said. "I guess we have a lot of catching up to do."

"We do!" I said, feeling my voice getting a little higher, like I was ordering something at an expensive restaurant. "I'm so glad we can do this!" My dying laugh again.

"What have you been up to?" he said, and I could feel his eyes on me. "I mean, how have the last twenty years been?"

"Well," I said, taking a breath, gathering all the confidence I had gained at the end of my twenties, "I'm a dance teacher. And I'm working on getting my own studio. Me and Laura are still friends! Her wedding is next month."

"No shit," he said, smiling. There was the swearing again. I had to remember he was an adult and I was, too. "You two were always so close. That's wonderful to hear." He was more impressed by the breadth of our friendship than my little, nothing career.

"It is, yeah. You know, it's *special*."

"I'll never forget when you killed the class tadpoles."

"Oh my God."

"It was kind of funny."

"I'm sorry, you thought that was funny?"

"I had to excuse myself. I was choking back tears just laughing." He started cackling then, clapping his hands together, his mouth open wide.

"Okay, that was literally so traumatizing," I said. My hands were a little sweaty on the steering wheel. I wiped them on my shorts.

"Come on, it probably gave you character."

"Probably."

"Do you like teaching?"

"I do."

"You seem to be doing well for yourself." He was just saying that. I glanced at my dusty Teva on the gas.

"I think so, yeah."

"Good for you." We passed by one of those billboards that said something about faith and salvation on it that could've been beautiful if it weren't so extreme and threatening. There was an easy-to-remember number underneath the proclamation.

"You think if we call 72-FOR-TRUTH, we'd really find out?" I asked him.

"Find out what?" Sometimes you realize that not everyone is looking at what you're looking at, that the things that light you up are what others simply pass by.

"If Jesus is alive!"

"Hmm, could be," he said. He was distracted.

"I always feel like everyone on the other end is randomly nice?"

"Most religious people are until you get a divorce or something."

"Yeah, my parents got excommunicated from our church because of that."

"I'm sorry to hear that."

"That means so much to me, Mr. Greco! Thank you! It's been so rough being away from the light of my Lord!" I looked at him sideways, and he laughed. We were nearing an area that had fences up along the highway for the deer. He asked me if he could touch one of my figurines, and I said, "Yes, please, help yourself." The car was my kitchen, and the figurines were all the snacks I had purchased for guests. He plucked up the Stitch figurine and held it in his palm, rubbed a small circle on the belly with his thumb. We passed by a sign, and I realized we were only a few miles away from Mike's, a chaotic dive bar I'd used to black out in during college before I went into my psychotic health phase.

"Do you drink?" I asked.

"I could drink," he said, smiling.

"Do you want to go to this cursed bar with me?"

"What makes it cursed?"

"You'll see."

Do you remember how we met Nick? I don't. I just have small memories from the beginning, and each small memory builds the door of the beginning, plants flowers around the entranceway: In fourth grade, a music teacher wouldn't let Courtney go to the bathroom, so she peed her pants, and then Nick accidentally put his hand in it (but did I see that, or did you just tell me?); in the winter, his lips got so chapped that they would turn green; in middle school, we all tried kissing, but with our thumbs over our mouths to not make it weird, and there were the little moaning noises he made, how I wasn't sure if he was imitating passion he had heard in porn or if he was just shameless, if he just wasn't like the other boys, embarrassed by the way he felt.

The bar had this sinister-looking cartoon painted on the front of it of a pig eating ice cream that had probably been something racist fifty years ago that they fixed only ten years ago. Inside there were mannequins everywhere and misshapen electric signs, arrows pointing nowhere. The menu was on a dry-erase board, and they had a bunch of alcohol but not a lot of food. The bartender had just started *Blade Runner* on the TV. The sun had started to set, and it cast a romantic light on the both of us. For another two hours, we would look our very best.

"I'll get this first one," he said, winking at me.

"Modelo for me, please! I only like the fancy stuff." I told myself I would only have two drinks max. I was driving, after all. I checked my phone. I'd texted you a meme about our astrology signs a few days before, and you hadn't responded—which I understood; you'd been busy. He came back with my Modelo and a Diet Coke.

"I have a horrible confession to make," he said, sliding into the booth. "I actually don't drink."

"Oh. I'm sorry. I didn't mean to drag you to a bar. Jesus, I'm sorry!" Should I have been worried that he was lying? He told me he could drink, but he never specified what.

"Please," he said. "You didn't drag me anywhere. I can still enjoy myself." I cautiously gripped my beer. He cracked his Diet Coke open.

"Will anyone else I know be at the wedding?" I wanted to tell him about Nick and how he very much wasn't going to be at the wedding. I wanted to see his face fall for me, the idea of somebody younger than him, somebody who had been my friend, dead.

"Do you remember Nick?"

"I don't," he said. "Tell me about dancing." He leaned forward. I knew exactly how the hair on his arm would feel under my palm, if I reached for it. A father's kind of hair. Like wheatgrass.

"It's just what I do!" I said, aware of my perfect posture and the calories bubbling in the beer in my hand. "I went to school for it, but then I dropped out. Now I teach kids free-form. Jazz."

"You've always had a spark about you."

"Thank you."

"I used to be a gymnast."

"I remember that. You were always doing, like, backflips and stuff."

"Right, of course you remember that. Sorry. Getting old." He scratched at his nose and cleared his throat. He was embarrassed. I was happy I couldn't see his sandals underneath the table, the earnest toes poking out of them. "I used to feel really alive up there on the beam."

"Like, you are most alive when other people are watching?"

"Sure," he said. "Yeah, I never thought about it that way." Chuckling and folding his hands, impressed with me, like we were teacher and student again and I told him that, actually, he spelled "beautiful" the wrong way on the whiteboard. But he would never spell "beautiful" wrong. On the screen behind him, Harrison Ford was meeting Rachael the robot, and she was reciting the memories they had implanted in her brain. Nobody was talking but us. I almost felt like we were being rude.

"My friend passed away a few years ago, and I did a show kind of dedicated to him."

"That's so sad, Andy," he said. "I'm so sorry to hear that."

"It's okay. It was healing. I curated together this track that had all these songs he liked that I actually hated, and then behind me I had really bad inspirational life quotes that said stuff like 'The way I see it, if you want the rainbow, you have to put up with the rain.'"

"Was that supposed to be ironic?"

"I think so." I could never tell if you really liked it. You said something after, when I was holding flowers my sister had brought me, that you weren't sure if I was a dancer or if I was a clown.

"Well, that sounds like an amazing show," he said. "I'm so sorry. Can I ask what happened?"

"Actually, he killed himself."

"Jesus."

"Yeah." His right hand turned over then, budded open for me to hold. I took it, and it was as dry as I wanted it to be, as warm.

"How are you feeling about it now?"

"It's been a few years. I don't know. Laura and I have been there for each other."

"I've lost a friend that way. It's tough." Do you remember how he used to give out pieces of his ties whenever one of us showed significant improvement in the week? I only ever got one sliver of a tie. It had little orange dogs on it that looked like balls of fire. It dried up in a box I kept under my bed. I don't know where it is now. One afternoon, after my parents had that nasty divorce and my father was nowhere to be found, my mom was three hours late picking me up from school. She rushed in at 6:00 p.m., coffee spilled all over her white blouse, apologizing in her accent and crying. She had been at work. She had forgotten about me. I was happily turning the numbers in my math homework into little people getting married to each other with a pink colored pencil. I remember her crying and crying, and Mr. Greco opening his arms and holding her. "It's gonna be okay," he said to her. "Everything will be all right." The next day, a piece of his tie was in my cubby.

Nick was the first white boy we fell in love with, and I think he started the parade of them. I imagine all of them lined up across the block, all kind of looking the same, shaggy-haired and broad-shouldered, ready to disappoint us. He was your first kiss (at the movies, watching *The Host*). He was also mine (at the Italian fair on the Egyptian boat ride, both of us screaming). One time we all sat on his battered couch watching *The Grudge*, and he was in between us, and I kept kissing him lightly on the neck, and you kept tapping his wrist with your pinky, and the movie simply ended, and we all simply broke apart.

And then after that horny, adolescent tension, we were all just buds, laughing until we couldn't breathe and running stoned through the high school football field. He burned us CDs. He made us read *Watchmen*. He walked us home when it got too dark. Everyone we introduced him to fell in love with him because he was so hot: tall and dark-haired, with a cow's eyelashes. Then we all went to college, and there was that year when I didn't see him but you did, and I had to hide my shock when I finally saw him in person at a Christmas party, fifty pounds heavier and almost balding. Is it wrong to say that, to even talk about it? His body?

There was a period of time when you and I were a little distant. In college I became health-obsessed after a back injury, only eating handfuls of Grape-Nuts and hard-boiled eggs as a vessel for my four hundred vitamins, and you became Kevin-obsessed, bringing him everywhere and changing all your opinions. I told you that he just looked like Nick if Nick were shorter and undeniably straight and kind of boring, which you were pissed about. "I've never been more certain of anything," you said.

After I was in recovery, comfortably eating sourdough bread and bowls of noodles, I got mad at you for saying that it was time for me to start thinking about holding down a real job. "You need to be realistic," you said. "I just worry about you sometimes." I said something mean to you about settling for somebody who didn't have a backbone and left your apartment without putting my socks on. A month passed by, and then you called me, and I answered on the second ring. You told me how they found Nick, how his girlfriend called the police because he had been missing. I thought you were joking. Later, when we were drunk and sobbing, you said to me, "I get it. I mean, it's hard. It takes so much to just go on." I didn't want to hear that. I wanted you to tell me that it was unspeakable and unimaginable, like the aliens that we have never seen and never will see because they're beyond the scope of our tiny human brains. Kevin made us tea and brought me an extra blanket and said he would sleep on the couch. That's when I started to like Kevin. That night we slept in your bed, holding hands.

"You are so pretty," you told me. "Except when you cry."

"I know," I said. "I look like Santa."

"Alcoholic Santa. Begging for his wife back."

"I don't really feel like joking right now."

"No, I'm sorry. I don't either."

"We can just be quiet."

"Okay."

"Actually, I don't like that either. It's scary."

"It is."

I got drunk at the bar. I know. I told him about my whole life, because he kept asking. I told him about my first boyfriend and how, after a few years, when he started to touch me, I would flinch, because the slow fade of romance turns lovers into siblings. I told him about the awful job I had at the dance studio in New York, with the boss who made me feel bad about eating bagels and almost made me spiral back into my eating disorder. I told him about the disorder, how I was never in danger but how I was in unrelenting control for the first time in my life, how I obsessed over foods that caused inflammation, how I could picture my body on fire from the inside. I told him about how my grandfather had died and I'd missed the funeral because I had an audition that didn't lead to anything. I told him about Vern, and how he was angry in ways I had been surprised about, that I only saw when we were all alone, so it made me feel like I was making it up. And Mr. Greco listened to every single thing I said. He reacted perfectly to everything, and of course he did. He was a third-grade teacher. He was used to bumbling idiots telling him horrible stories. A perfect audience is a perfect friend and a perfect teacher. I kept having more Modelos. The movie ended, and the bar got rowdy. For a moment, I saw something flash over Mr. Greco's face. It wasn't the malice you see in a villain's face in a Lifetime movie, that thing that makes your mom go, "See? I told you he was bad news." No. It was the awkwardness of a small boy holding in his pee, running past the face of an old man.

"Let's get out of here," I said, feeling my words collide into one another.

"I'll drive," he said. "Please, I insist." A few men in work boots at the bar were either getting into a fight or excited to see one another, pushing one another's arms and grunting with their rough hands. I asked him where he needed to be and when, and he said I shouldn't worry. It was the least he could do.

He was trying to get to Canada. I found that out later. They caught him at a motel near the border. They had tracked his laptop. He had all that shit on this laptop while he was with me. Can you fucking believe that?

This next part is hard for me. You're gonna judge me. I don't know when I am going to have you read this. It has to be after your wedding. You're gonna say, "I am calling the police," you're gonna put your head in your hands, and then you're gonna actually slap me, and I'm going to deserve it. And then what happens, Laura? What happens after that?

There is something erotic about being alone in somebody else's house, always. We've talked about this before. It makes you want to lie on the other person's couch and touch yourself. My professor's house was modern, intellectual, clean, probably a million dollars. Their cat, an orange fluffy thing, was waiting by the doorway, brushing her head against our ankles. Mr. Greco leaned down and held out his hand, which the cat sniffed then padded away from. Mr. Greco took off his blue sandals, and I tried not to look at his feet. I hated them, I decided. He was interested in the record machine by the giant bookshelf. There were loads and loads of books everywhere, in intentional places, and posters from old movies hanging in frames on the wall.

"I used to love *Dirty Dancing*," he said, slipping the record out of its sleeve and delicately placing it on the record player. Why used to? When did the love stop? The rattle and handclap of the first song began. I thought about how Nick would sing and how embarrassing it was. A low baritone that didn't ever match the mood. Like he was doing show tunes. Mr. Greco whistled along. I sat on the end of the couch and wondered how many years it would take to buy a place like this, or what kind of remote Republican town I would have to live in.

The couch was green and had velvet ridges on it that felt nice on my fingers. Mr. Greco had his hands folded in his lap and was staring ahead, the way he had been when I found him at the pie shop, waiting to be wound up. I watched his chest rise and fall as the song changed. I felt something pull at my groin.

"What do you think about me?" I asked him. He turned his head toward me and raised his eyebrows. I saw the small boy run across his face again. I was almost disgusted with him, how awkward he was.

"I think you're a remarkable woman."

"What else?" He laughed through his nose, little huffs leaking out of the holes in his face. He let silence sit between us, and it made whatever was pulling at me yank harder. Then he asked me where the bedroom was.

I had never been here before, but I assumed it was upstairs. I walked there, slowly, my bare feet thumping softly on the wooden staircase, my hand grazing the railing. *He is watching me move like a dancer*, I thought. *He is thinking what a woman I've become.*

I wondered if he would turn me around as soon as we entered the bedroom and kiss me hard, if we'd have many nights like this to come, if it'd fade out or end dramatically, if I'd be a sore subject for his future girlfriends, but something different shifted in the bedroom when he shut the door behind us. A fear grazed my arms, made the hairs raise. He told me to sit down on the bed. I did. He sat in a chair in the corner of the room. A photo of my professor and her wife and their son at an apple orchard rested on their bed stand. He told me to take off my clothes. I did. My body is still buoyant, after all. My tits are still small round doughnuts. He asked me if I thought I was a good girl. I said, "Sometimes." He asked me what I thought about when I touched myself. I said, "A lot of stuff." He laughed. He said, "Why aren't you more specific?" I told him, "Sometimes I think about women, but it's complicated. Tits in my mouth while a dick is inside me from behind. Filled all

the way up." He didn't even move. He just sat in his chair. That
didn't seem to be enough for him, so I told him that sometimes I
picture your face, but it almost appears as an intrusive thought.
It's like, I care about you the most, and I'm worried I will think of
you, and then I do, and then I burst. He shifted in his seat.
Mr. Greco told me to place my hands on my breasts. I did. He
said, "Good girl." I was wet. He told me to touch myself, so I did.
My breath was getting sharper. "Will you touch me?" I asked him.
He said no. He told me to pinch my left nipple. I did. He told me I
was making a lot of noise and I needed to cover my mouth. I was
my own burglar, my own man in the parking lot in the middle of
the night. My breath was hot and ragged against the inside of my
hands. I wanted him to kiss my fingers. I wanted him to tell me I
was the most beautiful woman to ever sit on a bed in Ithaca, New
York. He told me to keep going. He was stiller than a pond. He
was part of the chair. He was furniture that watched me back. I
came suddenly and shook and gasped. I realized I had been crying. He didn't say anything. His breaths were steady and even.
They never got faster. I felt faint. I knew my face must have been
bright red. He didn't break his gaze with mine. I had given something to him that I wanted to give away. I feared the moment he
decided to get up to go, because I knew I'd start to miss it,
whatever it was that I'd excavated from myself and handed to
him. But he did.

Lying on my back on quilted sheets, I waited for him to come
and kiss me. Instead, I heard the bedroom door open. I heard him

go down the stairs. I heard him lift the top off the record player and guide the record back into its sleeve. I heard him slip his backpack over his shoulder. I heard him click his tongue at the cat. I heard him open the front door and leave me, in the middle of the night, alone with an animal, in a beautiful house that would never be mine.

It was two days later, when I was scooping wet food out for the cat into a white porcelain bowl and waiting for my coffee to drip, that the police kicked down the door of his motel room twenty miles away from me and arrested him.

The day we killed the class tadpoles was the day that we became friends. You were entranced by a rock in the vivarium. It was almost a crystal. You loved the color of it. You wanted to touch it. I said I would get it for you. I reached in and scooped up the rock. I held it, dripping and jagged, in my tiny hands. It fell onto the floor, and you picked it up.

"It's heavy."

"Yeah!"

"I don't think I want it anymore."

"Okay." So I lifted it away from you and threw it back into the vivarium, where the tadpoles, who had just sprouted small legs, were crushed.

———

I am remembering something now, but who knows if I can trust it? We had gone back to visit our sisters, who were graduating from the fifth grade. We were fourteen then and starting to show more of our bodies. Nick was there with us but was outside by the playground, crawling into a yellow tunnel. We made fun of him for that. "Why is he obsessed with being indie?" we said. We didn't even really know what that meant. We saw Mr. Greco in the gym and rushed to say hi to him. I gave him a big hug, and when I moved away, he kept his hand on my shoulder. He had a stain under his armpits and a bead of sweat swimming down his face. He was flushed and breathing hard. Our sisters were singing a John Lennon song in a chorus and two-stepping with the rest of the class, back and forth, an ocean of little bodies waving. His hand didn't leave my shoulder until we did.

Mr. Greco is in jail. Thirty years. I stare at a photo of him on my phone with his hands in front of his face, handcuffs hugging his wrists, while the woman you hired applies blush to your face in the hotel room. It's six hours until you get married.

"Can you please do something with her?" You motion toward me and my flyaway hairs. The makeup artist comes toward me with her hands up like claws. I sit and let myself be made. Her touch is soft, and her voice is soothing. I could fall asleep like this. There's a knock on the door, and it's Kevin, holding a tray of Starbucks.

"Get the fuck out, Kevin!" I say. "No men allowed!" You give Kevin a peck, and he hands you a mocha latte. "Honestly, I love Starbucks," you say, plopping down on the bed in your oversized Built to Spill T-shirt. "I don't care if the whole world becomes a Starbucks inside an Amazon warehouse inside a Google Glass hallucination." You take a sip. "Really?" I ask. "Probably," you say. When the makeup artist finishes with me, turns me around in the swiveling chair for the big reveal, I look so beautiful that I feel like any sudden movements could wash it all away and I'll never look this beautiful again. I help you zip up your dress, and you ask me how you look.

"You are the most gorgeous woman to ever wear a wedding dress in a Holiday Inn."

"Thank you." And you hold my wrist for only a few seconds and then say, "All right, let's take these fucking pictures." The next few hours blur by. The poses out on the lawn in front of the venue, the heat making my back sweat, Kevin's cousin telling me to keep my knees bent at the altar to keep from fainting, the prewedding shots of tequila with friends from college. Suddenly I'm watching Kevin watch you walk down the aisle with your father. There's a small, sure smile holding up his face, and I become alcoholic Santa again, a blubbering, crying little bitch, because I love you. Because you are my greatest love story. Because I am slightly worried that I am going to be alone forever, in the traditional heterosexual sense, and I am worried that I am going to like it.

At the reception, Kevin's cousin's date, a tall, normal man with a gap between his teeth who works at some start-up that keeps you from looking at your phone, asks me how I spend my time, for money and for pleasure. I dab my mouth with a napkin, and I tell him that I teach children how to dance. He asks me if I ever want to do anything more than that, and I say, "Maybe, but I don't think I ever do." We are under a white tent, and it starts to lightly rain, then stop. I tell him I love how off rhythm they can be, how sometimes we don't learn a routine at all; I just turn something fun on the speakers, and they bounce up and down and run. Kevin's cousin leans in to listen, boob tape keeping up her cocktail dress. I wonder if he is bored with her, if he wants me to keep telling him about my chosen little life.

At a certain point in a long friendship, you envision every big life moment to come. Like right now, watching you introduce people to one another, your favorite thing to do, I am envisioning holding your baby and the speechlessness that I will feel, knowing that a person I've known my entire life has made an entirely new life, and the rush I'll feel to protect them, the fear I'll have that I'll chuck them across the room, and they'll break like a jar of jam. Nick isn't here, and I am happy we aren't people who think he is watching from up above. I am watching for him, anyway, but what version of him? The sad man who I stopped talking to in my early twenties, who I never visited in his new apartment that he hung himself in? The beautiful teenager who we both loved, who

I keep resurrecting in my head? We don't talk about him here, but look: the broken chair on the sprawling lawn, the early fall light tickling our sisters' faces in the lasagna line, a zipper on one of the groomsmen tragically undone, your diabetic aunt's sneaking a bite of cake—three white balloons just popped violently on their own, one by one. He's here, I think. If you really look. The DJ blasts a song by an artist with a problematic past, and all the guests, whether they like to or not, tap their fingers and bop their heads along. What if I got up, actually? God, I used to love this song. What if I asked you to dance?

Pobrecito

You're pissed with me because I'm telling the story again. I told it to you on our first date, and you were totally charmed: You gasped a little, almost choked to death on your pomegranate margarita. "I feel sick," you said. Kissing me later in my apartment, you broke away because you couldn't get the image out of your head. We stopped whatever we were doing so we could get some fresh air on my terrace, where we listened to dumb bros shout at a party in the apartment below. "It's just so sad, if you think about it," you said to me as the bros hollered at one another to *chug*. "Pobrecito," you said. You love saying that. You've said all good men are pobrecitos in some way. "Well, of course I've thought about it," I said, "that's why I told it to you." Now whenever I tell the story, you open your phone.

It's not like it's my only story or like other things haven't happened to me or people I know. It's just that it's my best one. So I'm telling it again, at our friend's book release party. She's more like your friend, though—I'm not her biggest fan. I think she's a ham who expects me to laugh at her jokes, but the jokes are all from the internet or about celebrities, so I don't understand them. She doesn't really care about me because I have nothing to offer her. I can see through that sort of thing. You hate when I say stuff like this. Right now, for example, she's doing that thing where she puts her hand over her chest like she's too in pain to say thank you. Come on. So performative. I'm standing with people who don't give a shit about me because, like I said, I have nothing to offer and work in tech and not publishing. We're talking about hometowns and the weirdest things that happened in them. I pour myself some of the free champagne, wait for the appropriate lull after a publicist says something about a tall owl in Albuquerque snacking on neighborhood cats, and begin, as if I've just remembered the story. Like it has just occurred to me after all these years.

Veronica was having her quinceañera. I'd always had a crush on her. I got invited to be a caballero with some of the other boys from high school. She had smooth skin and a face that was wide like the moon. She was always caked in Bath & Body Works cherry blossom soap. You wash yourself in this hypoallergenic Aveeno thing that you convinced me to use. Her parents were Mexican diplomats or something like that. All I remember is this: She was Mexican, and she was rich.

Because I was so short for a fifteen-year-old, they had her ten-year-old sister, Nemi, be my date. My mother was always worried that I wouldn't grow properly, and there was even talk of putting me on steroids to get me started. I eventually had a growth spurt on my own in my early twenties. I shot up to six feet, and hair started sprouting from my chest. Pretty shortly (ha-ha) after this, I kissed for the first time, then fucked for the first time, because finally I looked my age. Sometimes people think I'm older than I am, and sometimes it gets to me. That's why you're always telling me to rub all this stuff on my skin, even when it isn't summer. I'd only had six years of experiencing myself as someone desirable when I first met you on a dating app. You were so cute in your photos, in front of birthday cakes and bodies of water. You say my prolonged shortness is the reason why I am constantly working out. Why I don't cuddle with you in the morning or am too spent at night: because I'm too busy trying to be the man I never thought I was, at the gym and on bike trails and in rock climbing gyms. I think that's unfair. I think that's pejorative and using arguments your friends—who don't even know anything about us, by the way—make against me. Right now you're picking at the tiny tiramisu they're serving and slowly turning away from me to go talk to that guy who works with you in the graphic design department. What's his name again? Bart? I continue my story with my audience.

The other caballeros were my friend Terrance, Corey from math class, and Veronica's cousin Geronimo. That wasn't his real name; it was a nickname given to him, because that's what he would yell all the time. I don't even think he was her real cousin. Anyway, the family had given me a sword—a real, dull one—and

I kept wielding it around, but it made Nemi, the ten-year-old, wince. I kind of felt like her babysitter. My friends were laughing at me in a corner because I wasn't with a real woman. Turned out it wasn't the sword Nemi had to worry about. We took pictures together, my hands around her waist, which was tiny, because she was a child. In the glossy photos I was sent later in a CVS envelope, she looked bored and tired from how tight her hair was gelled against her scalp, the blue eye shadow heavy on her lids. It's weird that girls have to wear makeup that young. All for some stupid tradition that nobody even likes. You never had one of these things, I don't think.

Geronimo was annoying, I'll admit that. Some kind of neurodivergent thing going on. Not reading social cues, running around and making circles with his fingers, telling people they just got iced but not knowing how to follow through on that. Veronica's aunt kept yelling at him to calm down, and then he'd just give this evil grin and start running around again. He snuck up to Nemi and said, "I will kill you with a gun." She started to cry, and then he ran away with his hands up, like he was on a roller coaster, yelling, *Geronimo!* Veronica said he played too many video games. It took forever to get him inside the limo, where the boys were all on one side and the girls were all on the other. Corey sat with his legs spread so that they were touching mine. Veronica was very still and was trying to smile. I could tell she was trying to be happy. I could tell that she would do this again, in fifteen years probably, on her wedding day, trying and failing to feel the mythical euphoria of the very special day that marked her foray into late-stage capitalism. You are always saying sly things about marriage and engagement and children and how little time you have left. I can't tell if it's something you want or something that all your friends want you to want. When I tell you this, you ask me, "Well, what do *you* want?"

There's a sharp thud coming from outside the venue, and then a crackling sound. Somebody shouts something incomprehensible. People look at one another, trying not to seem too nervous. It's been a tense last year. Some of your friends have been sleeping with bags underneath their beds, in case anything happens. This morning you showed me something stupid on your phone, some video conspiracy about What They Don't Want Us to Know. It involved a weird object in the sky in Central America and then something to do with a leftist group one of your friends is in. I don't know. I wasn't really paying attention. I also hate it when you get your news from these places. You've turned your head toward the thud, the small scream. You laugh nervously at Butler or whatever his name is from the graphic design department. The last time we met, you were cagey about introducing us. When you talked to him, you looked at his teeth and then your hands, laughing even though he hadn't made a joke. And, look, it didn't make me feel jealous. I don't get jealous. I just don't want you to lie to me. I just want us to be honest with each other.

Veronica was trying to make everybody comfortable. She was self-conscious about the chaos of the day. I would be, too. It was a lot. She asked, "Should we open the roof?" The boys and the girls cheered, like, *Hell yeah, let's get crazy.* When you're in a limo, you do limo things. So she pressed a button, and the roof slowly opened. Of course, Geronimo wanted to stand out the sunroof. He climbed onto a seat with his dress shoes that were caked in mud from running around all day and stood up. He was whooping, hollering. Feeling so alive. "Careful," Veronica said. "Just be careful." But then she stood up with him, too, lifted her hands up to the sky. She was so beautiful in the afternoon light. I remember looking up at her, at the way the skin of her armpit folded in toward her small breasts, her pink dress billowing in the breeze, the glimpse I caught of her Hanes underwear. I think this is where my type began, if I have to be honest. I've never told you that, but you're smart. You like who you like.

There is some whispering happening now, all around us. People are shuffling toward the door. They're checking their phones. They're making calls. You're still talking to fucking Bernard or whoever, and he's having a bite of your tiramisu, and you're laughing. I'm remembering now how you were gone all last Satur-day after you had asked me about watching some new show I didn't care about, and I said that I had something else to do. I think I was mean about it because you told me you had to take a shower, which is a thing you do when you need to cry. Then you kissed me on the cheek, all happy, not talking about the new show anymore, and then you left for the whole day, and now I understand what you were up to, but I'm almost done with my story. Then I'll come and interrupt you. Then I'll ask you what, exactly, is going on.

Veronica came down and giggled, patting her hair, smoothing down her dress. Geronimo stayed up there, his hands up, yelling, once again, *"Geronimo!"* "Okay," Veronica said, looking up at him. "We're almost there. You should come down." But Geronimo didn't listen.

There's another thud. I wonder what floor we're on. Somebody just turned off the music. Your friend's talking to security. The audience around me is looking around to see where they should set down their drinks. "Hold on," I say, "I'm almost done." I know they'll still listen. They don't want to seem like people who get freaked out. People who are unreasonable.

———

Geronimo wouldn't come down. Veronica was tugging on his pant leg. He stepped on her and got all this mud on her perfect honey arm. I thought about offering her my tie to clean up. Be a gentleman. But I didn't. Anyway. There was a tree branch hanging low, and he didn't see it. And, well, then we heard a thunk. The slow roll of a head. His body fell backward into the car. The bow tie on his tuxedo was still fastened around his neck. I can still hear Veronica's screams and smell Corey's throw up on my legs, feel Nemi's nails digging into my arms. The limo screeched to a halt. We all had to make statements to the police.

I take one last sip of my champagne.

"I think I saw that in a movie already," the publicist says.

"No," I say. "Well, I know that. But it happened before already— to me."

"But it didn't happen to you," the publicist says, checking her phone. "You were just there." The publicist and the book influencer and the editor—my entire audience—make their way out the door, following everybody else. I am alone in the venue now. Something smells off in the air.

I find you outside, staring at the night sky, where something blue pulses above One World Trade. I can't describe the shape of it, but I can tell that it wants us. There's dust all around us from a crash. You always hated coming to this part of town. Said it was haunted. People are running. Barnie from graphic design has white all over his jacket. You didn't go with him. Did he leave you, or did you wait for me? People with handkerchiefs over their faces run past us with guns as the blue thing in the sky gets larger and larger. Your friend's floating in the air, her book event dress billowing and giving us all glimpses of her lacy underwear. She keeps rising and rising, her screams growing fainter as she flails closer toward the blue.

"I can't get in touch with my mom," you say, and your face is wet because you're crying, the way you do at movies or in the shower. The way you do all the time, and I can never at all. Everyone is leaving. All of publishing. All of every industry. And we're next, babe. You look at me and open your mouth, like you're going to confess something, about Barry or Brayden, or that you can see a life without me, that you've been picturing it so frequently that it's turned into an alternate reality, a place you think you can call home. But what's the point now? I bend over and kiss your forehead. You don't have to tell me about all that. You don't have to say a thing.

Heads

I find Tootsie's head in the lettuce garden, her snout open and her beady eyes, too. She's looking at me like I know something, like I've always known something, and it's just a matter of when that something bubbles out of me and grows legs. She was a little thing, a fuzzy almost-Chihuahua you could lose easily or sit on. I open the cotton purse with the purple flowers sewn onto the handles, grab Tootsie's head by the ears, and toss her inside. Blood leaks through the cotton. I have to tell Linda, and I don't want to. Linda's older. She's my friend. She was the one I ran to the night my father bashed my mother's head against the kitchen sink.

"I'm sorry," I say, holding up the cotton bag for her to see. "It's Tootsie." The heads don't bother me or make me sick; they just freak me out about the patterns of things and, when strung together, what everything can start to mean. Linda looks inside the bag and gags.

I see her eyes well, but she puts herself together, brushes her hands on her apron. "We had a few good years together, didn't we?" We don't talk about looking for the rest of the body. I follow Linda into her backyard, her flowered skirt billowing around her dry ankles. She limps slightly, dragging her left foot on the ground. She hands me a small red shovel, and I dig a hole in the yard we share. She throws the cotton bag with Tootsie's head into the hole.

"What do you think?" Linda says as I pat the dirt down with a shovel. "Is it that monster you're always talking about?"

"I wasn't going to say anything, but yeah. Is that crazy?"

"I've seen stranger," Linda says, sighing and looking out into the trees. The wind makes them dance.

"Shall we?" I ask. Linda's voice quivers as she begins, following the words of Ruth.

"'In this long life of shared pain, I found your soul, and you found mine. You were there, and so was I. We will work now, in your name, as you rest. Rest.'"

"'Rest,'" I repeat, placing a hand over my heart.

"Do you want me to ride with you?" she says, squeezing my shoulder. Today I turn eighteen. I'm now finally allowed to visit my father at the Halls, but I also have to decide how I'm going to contribute to the district. I haven't given it a lot of thought, though everybody expects me to just do Food Distribution with my Aunt Beatrice. I shake my head, focusing on the fresh mound of dirt.

"No, that's okay," I say. "You should relax." When Linda was still one of the head coordinators at Food Distribution at MA-13, she used to hold seventy pounds of groceries at a time. Then she tripped over a branch and broke her ankle. Our medics set it back, but it never quite healed. Some people think she was sabotaged, because you get extra rations when you're a head coordinator. Now rations get delivered to her every Tuesday and she doesn't have to work, which more people are mad about. I like that she doesn't work so much, because then I get to talk to her.

"So, what's the deal?" Linda says, her hands on her waist. "You afraid?"

"A little bit." I swap a fly away from my face. "Why? Do you think I'm self-centered?"

"I don't know why they have you thinking all these things. 'Self-centered.'" She shakes her head at the sky. "They think they invented piousness. Look, sweetie. You don't have to go. Nobody's making you."

"But I want to," I say. "I think the screenings helped. It's sad to see him in those rooms. I think he needs company."

"Those rooms look like my old college dorms!" she says, the skin around her eyes wrinkled petals. "I've seen them! Your dad is a lucky man." I rub one thumb over the other, like I'm trying to tell it to calm down.

"You'll be just fine, honey. Come back when you're done, okay? We can talk about it."

"Thank you." I pause. "I'm sorry about Tootsie."

"Not your fault, my dear. Not like you tore her head off!" She cackles and gives my hand a squeeze. I walk back to our living area, dead leaves sticking to my heels. My Aunt Beatrice chops wood in the back.

"There's blood all over the lettuce again," she says, the wood splitting easily into two. "Was there another head?" I nod.

"I'll write the street chat, ask them to keep a lookout for wolves. In the meantime, I'll cancel pickups from our neighborhood. No salads for a while." Aunt Beatrice lifts her axe again. The pieces of wood dive away from one another.

"What if it wasn't a wolf?" I offer. "What if it was a monster?"

"Mari, please. We need to get the wolf situation under control. Neighbors are in danger." She grabs another stump and sets it on the ground. The axe rises.

"How's Linda doing?" She twists the handle of the axe as it gets trapped in the stump. It breaks, and she keeps hacking.

"Still limping. It was Tootsie's head."

"Well, that's a shame."

She doesn't ask me about how I'm feeling today. She doesn't want me to go. When my mother was killed, Aunt Beatrice threw out all my father's clothes and burned them in the street's dumpster, wailing in a way I'd never heard before. A wail from the earth. From inside her blood. It was her one act of pain and the only form of vengeance she was allowed. She let me keep one photograph of him, where his eyes looked red and filled with blood. The rest she threw in the fire.

"Listen, I won't be home when you get back," she says, still hacking away. "There's a lot of nonsense happening in Education, and they need to me to mediate."

"Tonight?"

"Yes." I don't want to show Aunt Beatrice that I'm a little hurt she put her responsibilities before my birthday, because then I'll have to hear about being self-centered and how I don't even know how bad it was Before.

"Sounds good," I say.

"Have you decided what you're going to do?"

"No."

"You haven't given it a single thought? You're eighteen today, Mari." A "happy birthday, Mari" would've been nice.

"I wanted to decide at the end of the day. It's not like it's set in stone either."

"You don't have to do Food with me. You could always teach. You have me worried, talking about these monsters. Waste of time. What about composting?"

"I feel like I'm too disorganized for that." Aunt Beatrice kicks over another stump. I sometimes think my aunt is happiest out here, chopping away at dead trees. It's not that I don't want to do Food with Aunt Beatrice. Everybody has a role; that's what we're taught. Every life is precious, because everybody is responsible for keeping somebody else's life safe. I just never feel like it's my own life.

"Grab some, will you?" She throws the axe down and gathers the wood in her arms. Maybe because it's my birthday, she doesn't lecture me. I pick up a few blocks. One of hers rolls into a lettuce patch. She tosses the blocks to the side and shakes her head. She kneels and wipes blood off a leaf with her hand.

"Goddamn wolves," she says.

My bike's the only thing I have left of my mother. It's a baby blue two-speed that a mechanic in MA-11 helped me regear. I thought about being a bike mechanic because they get first dibs on what crops they want delivered, but the warehouse I went to had all these men, and I hate admitting this, but they made me blush. I pedal softly through my streets. I see Eva biking toward me with carrots in her basket. She's wearing a long-sleeved pink dress with built-in shorts. Her mother is the district's seamstress, and she always looks more put together than everybody else. The outfits I've been given for the season are fine, but Eva always looks like herself. It would be nice to look like myself sometimes. I don't even know who that is.

"Helloooo!" Eva says. "Happy birthday!" She remembered. I smile. "Where you off to, Mari?" We pedal together, our wheels buzzing in time.

"The Halls."

"Oh, *right!*" she says, her eyes growing wide. "How are you feeling about *that*?"

"A little freaked out."

"That makes a lot of sense," she says, and while she means it, I know she'll never relate.

"You started delivering today?"

"I did! But, oh my gosh, I got kind of confused with the spreadsheet. All the numbers. Maybe this isn't the right job for me." She giggles to herself. "I feel like Linda might be mad. But everybody has their place, right? That's what they say!" She giggles again. She's always giggling.

"Linda doesn't get mad," I say. Eva bikes ahead of me. Her curls are a breathing forest. Sometimes, as I fall asleep, I dream of myself colliding with the ground, pieces of my skull flying everywhere and turning into little white birds. I don't tell Aunt Beatrice about these dreams. We're pedaling together and pretty content with it, side by side, enjoying the beautiful day.

"I think I have a crush," Eva tells me, darting her eyes toward me mischievously.

"Oh?" I say, focusing on my spinning wheel. A pink flower got stuck and is getting squashed with each pedal.

"One of the gear guys," Eva says. "Who knows, he's probably—" Eva lets out a scream and crashes into a bush. The carrots roll to the ground. I leap off my bike and run to her.

"Are you okay?"

"You didn't see that?" she says. The skin on her knee's broken open, and blood's slinking out. I take the ointment I've packed out of my purse and kneel. She sucks her breath in through her teeth.

"What did you see?" I apply ointment, and she winces as the blood starts to bubble. I've already told Eva my theories about the monster, and she's been kind, but I don't think she really believes me.

"Thank you." I help her up, and she wipes the dirt off her skirt. "I don't know what it was," she says, picking up the carrots scattered across the road. "Whatever, I probably made it up. You didn't see it?"

"No."

"It was probably one of those wolves."

"Have you ever seen a wolf?"

"No."

"Then how do you know it was a wolf?" I'm being aggressive.

"I guess I don't know."

"Listen, Eva. I found a dog head in my lettuce this morning."

"Another one?"

"I feel like it's all connected."

"What is?"

"I don't know. All these heads. And that thing you just saw? I think something is going on. A conspiracy."

"Mari, I don't want to sound mean, but maybe you're listening to too many of those radio shows at night." I hand her the last of the carrots, and she can tell that I'm annoyed.

"Well, I better deliver these," she says, mounting her bike. "Thanks for the ointment. Good luck today."

"Whatever," I say. Eva pedals away, the carrots clapping together in her basket.

The Halls rest on the top of a hill, surrounded by mulberry trees. The teachers say that the Halls were an abandoned "elite" university after the rebuild. Now they house people you aren't allowed to see until you turn eighteen. A lot of care goes into these facilities, and some cynics think that neighbors will cause harm in order to get the Halls treatment, but who are they kidding? Nobody really wants to be there. I pedal while standing to give my thighs a little break as the hill swells. I reach the yellow brick building and set my bike in the tall grass. Inside, a woman wearing a yellow pantsuit sits behind a glass case. She has her hair slicked up in a neat bun. Behind her there's a golden banner that reads *WE ARE NOT WHAT WE HAVE DONE; WE ARE WHAT WE CAN BECOME.* I grab a mint from a bowl that's also golden, unwrap it from its yellow shell.

"I'm here to see Gabriel Ernez, MA-13."

She squishes her face into a smile at me. My father's face appears against the glass case, the reason why he's here, the night that it happened. I breath in, then out.

"You're his child?"

"Yes."

"It says today is your birthday?"

"Yes," I say.

"Happy eighteen years around the sun." She beams. "Do you know what you'll be doing? It's an exciting time."

"I'm not sure. Maybe teach."

"Oh, that's fantastic," she says. "You must be very patient. I never had patience, so that's why I'm doing intake. Plus I get time to work on my plays." She puts a finger to her mouth and points with another finger to the computer, like it is our little secret. It's not against the law to make art—it's often encouraged—but there's a series of tests to take in order to live as an artist in the artist commune, creating all day. Some of them paint murals on the schools; others make radio plays and broadcast them at night. The fact that she's working on her plays while at her designated job must mean she's not very good.

"That's cool," I say. "Can I go inside?"

"Oh," she says. "Right, of course." She presses a button, and the door next to the glass case opens. I'm met with a gush of cold air. This is the only place in our district that's air-conditioned. We just keep the windows open at home.

"Take a seat and help yourself to some food. We just got a delivery this morning. There's also some ice water." I walk through the doorway, and the door slips closed behind me. The waiting room is the color of butter, and the seats are cushiony, impeccably white, like the marshmallows we ate before they all ran out. I sit carefully in one of them, afraid I will dirty or break it. Beside me are a few other visitors my age, probably also here on their birthdays. We glance at one another and give little nods of understanding. There's a giant window looking into a sunny courtyard. There's a painting of three brown puppies nestled into one another like blankets. I look through the pamphlets on the cream-colored table next to me. One says *TALKING TO A LOVED ONE IN THE HALLS: SOME SUGGESTIONS*. I read through.

For decades the Halls have committed themselves to the rehabilitation of those who have Taken Life or Severely Traumatized the Lives of Others. Our patients undergo daily therapy sessions and have their choice of one to six "extracurricular" art activities. We have a gym facility for patients—

I fold the pamphlet into quarters and then unfold it, trying to smooth out the wrinkles and make it young again. I tap my foot. I stare at the puppies. I've been taken care of in this life. Aunt Beatrice read to me and stamped a kiss on my forehead every night. She said, "Love you," to me the way she also said, "Wipe down the counters," a hard afterthought, an ordinary direction. A lot of people grow up without fathers or even their biological parents. I am not special because of this. I've always had a community around me.

I hear my name get called. A person in white linen holding a clipboard calls me into an office. Suddenly I feel exhausted by all the steps of this, all the checking in, all the lights and the seats and the walls and the cakes. I take a seat in a red wooden chair. On this person's desk is a photo of them and another person, maybe the person's spouse, and a little baby.

"How are you feeling today about seeing your parent?" They fold their hands. They have long hair and gentle eyes, soft hair swimming across their arms.

"I don't know," I say. "I think, fine."

"That's good. I'll be in the courtyard the whole time. You only need to press this button on the pad"—they hand me a silver pad with a screen—"if you feel unsafe. Your parent has done a lot of work in his time here, so there should be no problem. You already know this, but there are no weapons here. Everything is built on trust."

"Okay," I say, fingering the edge of the screen.

"Happy birthday, by the way." They do not ask me what I'm planning to do.

"Thank you."

"Are you ready?"

"Yes."

They lead me down a hallway where more people in white pass us by, toward an open courtyard with an empty swimming pool.

"He's right over there," they tell me, pointing with their finger to a man sitting in a chair, looking out at the courtyard. It's the back of him. His curly hair's been shaved. There are his shoulders, broad like a mountain. There are the curly dark hairs peeking out of his shirt.

"I just go and say hi?" I can feel my shirt dampen from my armpit sweat. I wonder if it's possible to just turn eighteen next year.

"Yes," they say, "or whatever you feel is best. Are you okay?"

"I'm great," I say, taking one step closer. "I'm excited." I can see the puppies in the waiting room through a window, but from where I'm standing they look disgusting to me, a three-headed furry worm.

"Hmm," they say. "It's good to frame things that way. You sure you're all right?"

"Yup!" I say, swallowing. I take another step, and something inside me flies down a slope, turns, and crashes. I start sobbing. It's humiliating. All the blood in my body feels like it's in my face. I turn and run away.

My dad taught me how to ride a bike, but I can barely remember the moment now. I'm sure I was frustrated at first. I'm sure there were scabby knees and many tears. But I can remember all of us riding together in a line. My mother on her blue one, my father on his black one, me on the white standard children's one because I was small and still feel small when I drop a glass or have to hold in my pee. He must have had his hands on my waist, holding on to me like I was a loaf of bread, right before he let me go. It was before he started talking about conspiracy theories about the other neighbors and stopped sleeping.

I'm practically flying down the hill now. I cannot pedal fast enough. The mulberry trees blur past me as I make my way to familiar roads, thinking of my father's curly back hair and his graying head and Tootsie's pink open mouth and the puppies on the wall all nestled into one another like they were a single pulsing body. I stop at Linda's house, leaving the baby blue bike on the front porch. I knock on her door. She doesn't answer. I peer through the windows. Maybe she's in the kitchen.

"Linda?" I run to the back, where she keeps the key underneath a rug. I pass by the mound where Tootsie's buried and open her back door. I enter her kitchen, afraid I'll find her headless body seated at the table and her head dripping somewhere nearby. Something turns the corner, and I grab the red shovel by the door, but it's Linda, holding a small corn cake with a single wax candle in the middle. I've been told that you used to light it and then blow it out, but it isn't worth wasting the oil now. Eva is behind her, her hands clasped together, smiling. They start singing together and clapping, and I drop the red shovel. Eva jumps up and down, and Linda sets the cake on the table.

"Make a wish, sweetie!" Linda says, gently arranging my hair away from my face. I close my eyes and blow on the candle, imagining a flame I extinguished with my breath. "What were you gonna do with that shovel, Mari?" Linda laughs and so does Eva, and I find myself laughing, too, for being so ridiculous.

"I'm sorry. I had a weird morning." Eva turns on her heel and rushes out the door. She's probably sick of hearing about this. I get it.

"How did it go?" Linda rummages through her kitchen cabinets and then takes out a small knife.

"I couldn't do it." She cuts the cake into three even pieces, picking one up for herself.

"Aw, honey, it's okay. No one's blaming you." I bite into my piece, trying to concentrate on its sweetness and not how guilty I feel. Linda wraps her weathered hand over mine.

"You didn't know how you were going to react until you did. It takes time."

"I saw the back of his head, and I thought about Tootsie's head, I think? I don't know." A sigh from Linda. She sucks her fingers when the cake is done and smiles at me. She looks all worried, the same look everyone has given me since my mother died, like there's something inside me that's gonna mutate and grow on the walls.

"They had a portrait of dogs in there." Linda leans forward and knits her brow. Even if she doesn't believe me, she's interested in what I'm saying, like it's the plot of a radio story. There's times when I wonder if that's what I should do. If I should join the bungalows and write elaborate stories with other artists. But I can never think of anything good. Everything is recycled from something a little better. And I think some people need to be the ones who listen, and it's okay if that's me.

"Go!" I hear Eva say, and I hear little nails scratching against the floorboards. A chocolate-colored puppy runs all over the kitchen and jumps on Linda, licking her face. Another puppy in a day of puppies. Strange.

"You got Linda another dog? After this morning?" I'm defensive.

"The dog's yours to take care of, silly," Linda says, and the puppy leaps off her and waits at my feet. I hold out my hand, and she licks it.

"I found her on my delivery route today," Eva says. "My parents are allergic, and nobody can take care of her. She's yours." Remembering that nothing belongs to us, Eva corrects herself. "Yours to take care of." The puppy chases her tail. I'm envious of her. She doesn't know anything about anything.

We take her out into the shared yard, and I'm amazed by how fast she goes, her legs taut and muscular, built to run and catch things and bring them to us. She knows what she's always been meant to do. She doesn't even have to think about it.

"How was today?" Eva asks me, wrestling a rope from the puppy, the puppy making aggressive play-noises at her.

"It was fine." I don't tell her anything else.

"I heard it's really nice in there," Eva says, the puppy gnawing at the rope. I feel Linda's eyes on me.

"So nice," I say. Eva smiles. I wonder what it's like to be her. She doesn't know what kinds of questions to ask because this hasn't happened to her.

"Oh darn," Eva says, looking at the sinking sun, "I have to go. My dad wants us all home for dinner. He's a little nervous."

"About the monster?"

"The wolves," Eva says, not meeting my eyes. Linda gives Eva a hug.

"I'm sorry, sweetie," Linda says to me, "but I have to get going, too. It's our monthly neighborhood check-in meeting." I make kissing noises at the puppy, but she doesn't know that that means to follow me. I feel really lonely all of a sudden.

Eva waves goodbye to me from her bicycle, and I watch her pedal away. Shadows stretch all around our house. The puppy runs ahead of me, sniffing the porch and the door. She rushes inside when I open the door, sucking the entire history of our house up through her nose.

On the counter there's a new delivery basket with a note from Aunt Beatrice. *I'll be back home later. There's chicken in the icebox.* The puppy nestles into a ball on our old blue couch, and I think once again of the painting at the Halls. I shut the windows. I turn on the radio and listen to a drama about space and time travel. Nobody goes to space anymore. The world is smaller,

and it is better that way. I listen to the news. Medicine develop-
ments. Another year of climate catastrophe delayed thanks to
No Cars. A group of ability activists asking to make the wagons
for those who can cycle more comfortable, pushback from
mechanics who need the resources to fix bikes already in use.
The sentiment from everyone is that at least it's better now. I
take the chicken from the icebox and make a fire outside. I fry
the harvest of okra and mushrooms in lard we have stored, still
fresh from the delivery on Tuesday. I make a list of things I can
do with the rest of my life. I cross them all out. In the trees I see
two red lights. I blink, and they're gone. I think I'm seeing things,
just putting together a story to make myself feel better. The
drama on the radio ends. The astronauts make it back home. It's
a happy ending, but it turns out one of them isn't an astronaut at
all. He kisses his wife good night as a stranger and, as a stranger,
turns off the lights.

"Puppy," I say, "let's go to sleep." I climb into the bed I share
with Aunt Beatrice, think about energy preservation and how it is
best to keep the lights off, but the radio drama scared me a little
bit. So maybe I can deal with Aunt Beatrice yelling at me when
she gets home, in exchange for being at ease. The puppy jumps
into bed with me, but I don't want to get her started on bad habits,
so I place her on the floor. She jumps back up. I put her back on
the floor. We go back and forth like this until she gets the point
and gives in to the floor. I hold out my hand to let her lick it. Her
tongue is warm. I do this every five minutes until I dream of the

puppies in the photo, swirling and gnawing at one another's tails, swallowing one another's heads.

I wake up. The lights are all still on. I don't hear Aunt Beatrice anywhere. Where is she? I hold out my hand for the puppy to lick it, and she does, her tongue warm and comforting. I'm fine. I'm safe. Aunt Beatrice will be home soon, and then I'll wake up to her snoring.

When I roll over, the puppy is next to me in bed, her small body rising and falling as she peacefully snores. Who was licking me? I twist my body and slowly inch toward the edge of the bed. I lower myself slowly, so slowly that it's almost painful. I try not to breathe. When I see the two blinking red eyes in the darkness, I freeze. *It's come for me*, I think. I leap back up and grab the puppy, slamming the door shut and pushing a flimsy chair in front of it. When the door rattles, I run with the puppy into our closet in the hallway. The puppy is growling, and I hold her snout closed with my palm. "Shh," I say. I hear heavy breathing and that awful nail-scratching and know I'm not crazy. I know it's not a wolf. I see its shadow beneath the door, it's breath rattling. It almost sounds like it's laughing. Then it lets out a horrific howl and dashes away, nails scratching against the floor. I hear glass break.

There must be a reason why I am the only one finding the heads, on this day of all days. I remember my dad's curly back hairs. I keep my dad's photo in this closet, in an old shoebox of memories. Red eyes, staring up at me. So it is him, after all. Does that mean whatever is in him is in me? Everything comes together for me suddenly.

I move our jars of pickled vegetables and find the pad installed in the wall. I dial Eva first. Her face flashes before me. She looks sleepy.

"Hello?"

"Eva. Can you come over here?"

Eva yawns. "Why? What's up?"

"You know that thing you saw earlier today? Did it have red eyes?"

"I don't know. It was in a tree."

"I think it's trying to tell me something."

"Like what?" Eva's eyes get bigger.

"I don't know. Something about . . . I think it's my dad."

"What?"

"I think my dad turns into a monster. I think he sneaks out from the Halls."

"To kill dogs? Mari, what are you talking about?"

"I already told you."

Eva's silent on the other line.

"Hello?"

"I'm just worried about you," Eva says.

"Well, I'm only calling you because I need to call someone before I press the green button. So thanks for being that person."

"The green button? That's for emergencies."

"Goodbye, Eva."

"Mari, wait!"

———

I hang up and move my finger to the upper right hand of the screen, where the green button lives. My hand shakes. I haven't pressed the green button since the night my mother was killed. And even then Linda did that all for me. The screen asks me if this is a life- or limb-threatening emergency. I click yes. The screen asks me if there is anyone in my immediate surroundings who can help me. I look at the puppy, who is licking her asshole, and click no. The screen asks me if I have reached out to someone I can trust with this information. I click yes. The screen asks me if this person can help in the immediate situation. I click no. The screen asks me if I remember the laws of our district, which state that you can only press the green button if you are completely helpless and cannot defend your own life. I click yes. The screen asks if I am ready for the process that will follow for pressing the green button. I click yes. It asks me for my birth date and the code for the screen. I type it in along with the code: my mother's birthday. The screen begins counting down from ten, the electric numbers blasting my brain awake. I hold my breath. I bite my lip, chew on the dead skin.

A slow jingle begins down the street, then gets louder and louder. *There will be drama*, I'm thinking. *There will be neighborhood gossip.* But this is normal. This is just the system working. The puppy and I are in the living room, and I'm holding the red shovel as protection. She's running around in circles, chasing her tail. Our window's been broken, and a piece of bloody fur sticks to the edges. That'll be good. Evidence. They'll believe me. They knock on the door, and the puppy runs to it, happy to greet strangers. I try to feel confident and reasonable. A knock on the door. I'll explain to them what I explained to Eva, and they won't think I'm crazy or somebody who causes harm to others, and they won't stick me in a courtyard, waiting forever to die. When I open the door, the responders are all in white, their bikes parked on their stands in a little line. One of them carries a bag, which I know holds tranquilizers. A tall man with a hefty beard clears his throat.

"We are here because the green button was activated. We will not use force unless there is an immediate threat. My name is Neighbor Gary, and the person holding me accountable is Neighbor Lauren. This is Neighbor Jan, who will activate sleep serum, but only when necessary. What is the problem, neighbor?" The puppy's at my heels. She growls.

"My dad is in the yard, and he's trying to hurt me." The puppy barks. I know I can't say "monster" because they won't believe me.

"Your dad? I see. Neighbor Lauren, please pull up the information we have on this house."

Neighbor Lauren takes out a remote, then clicks a yellow button, which shoots out blue light with information into the air between us.

"Residence held by Beatriz Fallon of MA-13. Cynthia Ernez, life taken by Gabriel Ernez on October twenty-first, ten years and two months ago. Ernez has been residing in the Halls for ten years. Are you Marisol?"

"Yes."

"It says it's your birthday, Marisol."

"Yes."

Neighbor Jan adjusts his backpack of tranquilizers and seems to pick his wedgie. This is who is supposed to help?

"Really exciting time. Do you know what—"

"Not now, Jan."

"Sorry."

"Where did you say you saw your father?"

I bring them to the yard. The puppy follows at my heels. They turn on their flashlights, and the light washes over the yard.

"I don't see anybody here."

"Neighbor Gary is not believing Marisol, the neighbor who pressed the green button." Neighbor Lauren speaks into a recorder.

"I'm just stating facts, Neighbor Lauren. There is nobody here."

"Neighbor Gary must take all measures to see if Neighbor Marisol is safe."

Neighbor Jan pets the puppy's stomach and smiles. She rolls onto her back with her tongue out, legs wiggling in the air.

"Cute dog! What's her name?"

"No name." I scoop her up and hold her to my chest. I'm surprised by how protective I am of her.

"I had a dog once. But unfortunately—"

"Jesus." Neighbor Gary shines his light on the lettuce patch. "These are some good heads of lettuce here. Really round. Do you have a secret for planting them? Ours always get worms."

Suddenly I feel stupid for pressing the green button. I should've just gone back to sleep. These people can't fucking help me. I'm a stupid idiot girl with an active imagination. Neighbor Gary searches the length of the yard. He walks toward the corner of the garden.

"What do we have here? Oh no. I've been hearing reports about these little guys." Neighbor Gary is holding up a cat's head by the ears. Then he gasps. In this moment, I hate that I'm right. A yellow claw shoots out of Gary's stomach and pulls back, squirting blood everywhere. Neighbor Gary grabs at the insides spilling out of him as blood dribbles from his mouth. The monster knocks him to the ground and begins to feed. I want to move, but I can't. I want to scream, but I can't. Neighbor Jan shakily takes out the tranquilizers but drops them. He faints. Neighbor Lauren drops to her knees and vomits, spewing her delivered harvest onto the grass. Her screams drill into my ears, and I see my father again, wailing on the floor next to my mother's lifeless body. I see my Aunt Beatrice throwing my father's things into the fire. I see the wooden box that held my mother being lowered into the dirt by the gardens as we say the words from Ruth, where her body will eventually feed the soil, which will birth fruit, which will go later into our mouths. I know it's wrong to think of people as innocent or not innocent. Neighbor Gary is innocent. Was innocent. He's dying, anyway. He's dying, and it's my fault. I hold the puppy to me as she barks and barks.

"S-s-stop," I say to Puppy and to the monster pathetically.

What's eating Gary is enormous. Its hair bristles, almost jiggles. Its fly eyes flick red and in all directions. Hard nails sprout from ten humanlike fingers, protected by brushes of fur. I don't know why it has to survive this way, feeding like it will never again. I hear a final "please" from Neighbor Gary, and then his hands fall slack behind him. The hard fear on his face fades slowly, an old photograph, as the monster gnaws away at the meat of his neck, snapping his head off like it's a button. The monster lets out a growl and then a huff. This is it. This is how it ends. Neighbor Lauren backs away on her hands, standing up and stumbling again, dragging Jan by the collar. "Get up!" she says. "Get up!" What have I done? I'm thinking that the lettuce will surely be ruined now when I hear another yell. An otherworldly scream. It's Aunt Beatrice, running, flying practically, with her axe. She hacks into him.

"Damn you!" she says, shrieking, the blood showering her. "Damn you, damn you!" I've never seen her more alive, sinking the axe into the monster's neck. The monster's caught off guard. The monster had no idea what was coming.

The jiggling stops. The bug eyes flutter close, blankets in the wind. It crashes to the ground and stays there. I wait for it to turn into a man, somebody I know, but it doesn't. Its mouth is open the way Tootsie's was, pink, wet, gaping. It licks its lips and wheezes.

If it weren't right before me, if I were all alone outside in the woods and could sense something close to me, I would've thought it was crying.

I'm told they brought the body to the medic quarters. That they sliced it open at the navel. They pulled out organs that resembled ours: a stomach, a heart, a loopy intestinal tract. They peeled back its eyes and stuck a tube down its throat. I'm told they had never seen anything like it before. They asked me if I wanted to have a look; I caught it, after all, or rather, I was the one who pressed the green button. I didn't want to. It was enough to know that I was right. And besides, I wasn't raised to take credit for anything. I'm told that somebody, probably someone new to the job, wrapped the monster's body in cloth and then set fire to it, waited for it to turn to ash, that there's an ongoing investigation with the Department. Our district hasn't seen an animal head in over a year. Everybody is as safe as they've ever been. Aunt Beatrice never really talked to me about that night. She hadn't really been mediating an argument in Education; she'd been grabbing a bell from another district for my bike, for me, as a present. The bell was golden, and when you flicked it, the noise wasn't shrill or abrasive but light and pleasant, like it was saying "good morning" instead of saying "get out of my way." She gave it to me wordlessly, in a small pink cup. She isn't one for gifts because she thinks they make us forget our commitments to one another, but I think sometimes they're for helping us remember someone when they're gone. When she arrived, her instincts simply set in, and after she was done killing it, she dropped the axe and held on to me in a way she never had before, like she was trying to squeeze all the bad out of me. Later I tell her my secret theory, the one about how it was the monster who'd killed my mother all those years ago.

"That's certainly a theory," she tells me.

"But don't you think it's weird that I was the only one finding the heads? And that my mother died in a similar way? I mean, what if Dad was framed—"

"Similar? Your mother's head wasn't missing, Marisol. Let's talk about this another time. I'm tired."

"And then there's the thing about the red eyes. The picture I have of my father—"

"Marisol, that's how pictures used to be. It's a trick of the light."

"You never want to hear what I have to say! I was right about the monster. Why can't I be right about this?" Aunt Beatrice sprays the counters again, even though they look clean to me.

"Get the mop," she says, not looking at me.

"Why don't you talk to me?"

"Get the mop," she repeats. She fills up a bucket with water and adds two drops of apple cider vinegar and soap she made earlier this week. I shove the mop in and think about how it looks like a woman upside-down, drowning. I dance the upside-down woman all over the kitchen floor while Aunt Beatrice dusts the cabinets. She opens them up and wipes down our dishware, the two plates we share between each other. The sun goes down, so I go outside and gather some blue flowers that have just started blooming. I cut them swiftly with scissors and place them in a jar of water. I set them on the kitchen table, where Aunt Beatrice is polishing the silverware. I think I see her bottom lip trembling, little flecks of water hitting the spoons.

Puppy got bigger, and she stays by my side. It's taken me a while to go back to the Halls. An entire year. Over the year, my hair has grown a little longer. Linda's ankle never improved, but I bring Puppy over to her every day, and she teaches her simple commands: paw, sit, play dead. I've ignored incoming calls from my father. Eva started working there as an intake specialist. I never apologized to her about freaking out over the phone, but we are close enough that some things are understood, and then they fade. I think it's a good job for her. Today's my birthday again. Nineteen. Tomorrow I start with the mechanics. I am not self-conscious anymore. I take my bike to the Halls as I did only a year ago. I lock my bike in the pod again. I open the door again, but this time it's Eva sitting there. I don't know what happened to the girl who writes plays. Maybe I'll be listening to the radio sometime and recognize her voice, and it will be like our secret, because I knew her before she was good.

Eva sits with me before I see him. She moves her foot around in a circle. Her ankle is brown, bony, and tender. She bumps her shoulder against mine to tell me that she is here.

My dad is right where I left him a year ago, as if only seconds have passed since I ran away. For me the year was filled with movement: the puppy running into a full-grown dog, the leaves shaking yellow, then dying beautifully, then blooming green again, my hairs branching apart at the ends, but how does he tell time? What changes in the Halls? I never want to wait like this. I never want to be this still. Seeing the back of his head, shaved and gray, sends something down my spine again, a messenger, maybe, a person with a bag full of letters all screaming "HELP!" The dog's by my heels, panting. We walk to him together. My hands shake. I take a seat next to him, at a white table that is just starting to rust.

It's strange seeing my father like this. Like somebody stuck him through some vat of aging juice, and he came out on the other side. I guess that's time. I guess we're on the other side before we even know it. He is only feet away from me. It's the closest I've been to him since that night. I forgot that his eyes are like mine: a deep brown. A deer's eyes.

"Marisol," he says. "My Marisol." He stands up, the chairs squeaking away from him. I see the therapist stand up from another table, just in case he tries anything. You are never really alone here. My face is wet. He opens his arms, and I find myself in them. My dad. One half of all of me. He lets out a low moan that almost sounds like a laugh, and my heart is wrapped tightly in string and desperately yanked. We pull apart. I wipe my face, and he wipes his.

"And who is this?" he says, looking down at the dog.

"That's the dog." Puppy has her tongue out in a smile. He sticks his hand down, and she runs to it, sniffing. He picks her up with ease, not even thinking about it. He is smiling in a way I've seen myself smile in pictures, as if he just drank a bunch of water and is about to laugh. I am caught up in this moment. It bursts away from the circumstance it was born from; it stands alone and shivers. I want to hold it forever and keep it warm. But there's a reason I came here.

"Dad, I need to ask you something." He's holding the dog like she's a baby, patting her back as she licks his face. He laughs at her touch.

"Yes, my love. Ask me anything."

"Did you hear about the monster who was taking heads of animals and, um, people sometimes?"

"I think so. There was something about it in the weekly briefings. Why?"

"Well, I don't know if you know this, but I caught it, technically."

"Did you? Well, I'm very proud of you, honey."

"Yes, um. So, something else I wanted to bring up is—" The puppy licks my father's face wildly. He seems so happy. So happy that he isn't even paying attention to me. I clear my throat.

"Something else is, um . . . I just think it's funny or it's interesting . . . I think it's interesting that . . . that it's similar to . . . well, the monster. I sort of think . . . I sort of think the monster killed Mom that night." The smile on my father's face falls. He gently brings the dog down.

"Mari."

"The monster that overtook you that night. Or the government implanted something in specific groups of people to turn them against one another so that we would never rise up again." My heart is racing.

He lets out a deep breath of air. He scratches his head. The dog's still at his ankles, begging to be picked up again. She whimpers. My father's hands, two rakes, scratch the dog's thin neck as an instinct. He sees me watching, so he takes his hands away, folds his fingers gently together in his lap. I cross and uncross my legs, the chair making a little squeaking sound as I do. He inhales. I exhale. He looks at me again with his deer eyes that are mine. There are stretches of land between us, an abandoned, sloping highway we would sled down on garbage pails in the winter. The dog barks.

"Come here, baby," I say to the dog, holding out my hand, making little kissing sounds. She looks up at me and then at my dad and then back at me again, tongue out, smiling. "Come here," I say.

The Heiress

The Colombian heiress had problems of her own, obviously. Traumas I couldn't relate to. She was very stressed out from writing her thesis on the economy of Colombia and the way it was affected by riots on the coast, as well as feeling like she was trapped inside all day. Her parents kept strict eyes on her, always worried about her diabetes and her taking the train. There weren't many accessible stations, so she got everywhere by car. Her assistant, Jorge, came in and asked us what we wanted for lunch.

"The usual, porfis," she said. I always worried that one day, there would be no lunch, that she would send me home early and starving, but there was always, always lunch: large sandwiches from Cardullo's, stuffed with prosciutto and cheese and arugula, bathed in olive oil. I'd have one half with the Colombian heiress and then have the other for lunch the next day. I almost can't look at the photos of myself from back then. I was so skinny. I practically got off on survival, as if living in New York City on my own was like climbing a mountain every day for a chance at sipping water. I feel envious of that previous me, but also concerned for her and the bones stretching against her skin.

That day, we were going over an essay she needed to finish for her comp lit class. I had taken most of the notes for her, and she just needed to write out the paragraphs.

"This is so boring for me," she said. "Can we take a break?"

"Sure," I said, closing my used Mac. She took out a baby pink vape and sucked from it like it was a bottle. She offered it to me, and I declined.

"What do you want in this life?" The vape smoke smelled like unicorn farts.

"I don't know," I said. "I just take it one day at a time, I guess." With her, I spoke in American idioms found above fireplaces in summer homes.

"So smart," she said. "You say the most beautiful things to me." Her eyes were giant pools. Jorge returned with the sandwiches. I ordered mine with spicy sauce. She did not. I thanked him, and he bowed away.

"Do you have a therapist?" the Colombian heiress asked, biting into her sandwich. We sat by the giant bay windows. I shook my head, blocking my sandwich-filled mouth with my finger. I'd recently had to stop seeing mine because I couldn't afford the eighty-dollar co-payment. In the years that would follow that day,

I would spend a few semesters' worth of money on therapy, waking up in the middle of the night screaming, breathing in too much air, and taking propranolol to slow my heart rate.

A white van pulled up on the street below us. Spring was coming, and with it, the small sadness that I hadn't been as productive as I could've been in the winter. The alarm on my phone went off. I had forgotten to charge it while I was here.

"All right," I said, "I gotta bike home."

"Do you hate me?" Tears brimmed in her eyes.

"What? No, of course not."

"I am just so bad with these school things. You are so helpful." She sniffed.

"I don't hate you. Really. I just have to go now. I have plans." I didn't.

"I can have Jorge make us micheladas. We have beer."

"Aren't you gluten-free?" She tsked and flicked her hands at me. Of course she had gluten-free beer. Or just didn't care about the repercussions.

"Stay with me." I did. The micheladas were spicy and sweet. Jorge served them to us with a wink. Pushing the cuticles back on her nails, she said, "Sometimes I feel so empty. I want something to happen to me. I thought we were in the big city. Harry meets Sally. I want to fall in love." She asked me if I was in love, and I told her yes, even though I wasn't technically in love with Lawrence anymore. He'd texted me a video last month in reference to something I'd once said about pineapple on pizza. I formed a message and didn't send it because I was so depressed thinking about the ten or so banal messages that would pass between us.

"Thank you for stay with me," she said. "I needed this. We will do it again." I pulled my jean jacket over myself. She gasped.

"You need a coat," she said. "It's cold. Jorge! She needs a coat!" Jorge came with a pink fur coat held up by his hands.

"You can have," she said. "Is my gift to you."

"That's okay," I told her. "Plus I'm gonna get it sweaty from biking."

"Take it. I have too many."

I stepped out of the apartment building and down the steps, opening my phone to see that it had died, and then—everything went black.

I woke up in the back of a van with a rag in my mouth.

"Is she awake?" I heard them say in Spanish. "Wake up," they said in English.

"Are you sure this is her?"

"Yes, look at the photo."

"But I thought she had no legs."

"She has legs; she just can't use them."

"No, she can't use *one* of them."

One of them touched my ankle, and I shook it away. Then the other ankle. I shook it away.

"We got the wrong one."

"Well, now, what do we do with her?"

"Get rid of her." They took the rag out of my mouth, and I tried to scream, but all I let out was a little whimper, a tiny clock chiming. One of them wrapped his hand over my mouth.

"Take her," I heard them say. "And take care of her." They shoved a pillowcase over my head, and obviously, this was when I thought I was going to die. A hand led me by the wrist as I stepped over rocks. I can still smell it now. I can still feel the saltiness on my skin.

"Are you going to kill me?" I asked, feeling a cold pistol through my T-shirt. The man said nothing. I sighed. I was weirdly calm, which I've heard happens at the end of your life. You can't survive anything if you're freaking out. "Are you going to kill her?" He was still quiet, but I heard a sniffle. Was he crying?

"You don't have to," I said, feeling bad for him but also feeling like I was on the edge of a very tall building. "Nobody knows me. I'm just a tutor. I'm literally moving in a week." That was a lie. I wouldn't move for another year, with Lawrence, a few months after we would reconnect, when his mother died. "I could move tomorrow!" Another lie. I felt the gun leave my back. Through the pillowcase, I saw little ideas of light, cars and buildings and e-bikes and boats, all these things that make a city. I felt the pillowcase lift off me. We were facing Brooklyn. I turned slowly and saw a short guy with a shaved head and a yellow handkerchief over his mouth. I could see the muscles forming like packaged produce beneath his white T-shirt.

"Ransom?" I was so unbelievably calm. Later, when I would finally get home, I would throw up in my toilet and fall asleep on the bathroom floor, crying.

"I won't tell anybody," I said, looking down at my hands, dry and weathered from biking all winter. He looked toward me. He had deep brown eyes that were a little close together and lived in dark, sleepy sockets. *There's so much I haven't done*, I thought, looking at a squashed water bottle with bits of orange floating around the bottom. Vitamin C mixed up with spit. I waited for panic to come, but it didn't.

"What if we went on the ferry?" I said, my last resort, my emotions blunted by a need to live. A train passed below us. I knew exactly how to bike home from here. Maybe I could run. But that didn't mean I wasn't in danger. He made a move with the gun and I flinched, but he was just opening my backpack, which was once pink and had now turned a scabbed-knee color from my sweat. He placed the gun in the backpack and threw the backpack over his shoulder. His eyes darted to me. He was just a kid, I realized.

"So, yes?" He was clutching onto the straps of my backpack, which held the gun that could've blasted a bullet through my skull. He gave me the slightest nod. Really, it was more of a twitch, but the twitch showed me that I was in charge now. A few worries pulsed through me: Would he rape and kill me if he felt like I was leading him on, was I being xenophobic thinking that, was I being naïve *not* thinking that, was it self-centered to think someone was going to rape me, why had he suddenly changed his mind? I was young, but I wasn't an idiot. I was just trying to survive.

"Okay," I said, "well, come with me."

It wasn't weird for him to be wearing a face covering because of the times, so I fastened mine on as well. We just looked like two people walking into an establishment politely. I bought us two tall Modelos and made a joke about how he should technically be buying because this was a first date, but he didn't laugh at that. I talked to him in jilted Spanish that had been improving from my time with the heiress. Not because we spoke it to each other, but because her intonations had bled into mine. I could be singsongy, have a personality. In the light of the deli, I noticed his forehead and the lack of wrinkles around it. I guessed he was Central American, just because of his height. I thought about all the things that had collectively brought us together: our mothers sweating on hospital cots, afternoons spent watching teen stars make the Disney sign with green lightsabers, the way travel was forever changed after 9/11, recessions, adult cartoons. But I wanted everything to have meaning back then. He probably hadn't had cable.

We walked to the docks, looking like tourist siblings. Like we had both just arrived and were trying to see what it was all about. I tried to make more small talk with him, but he refused, so I eventually gave up and decided that our legs walking slowly in time was conversation. We had a silent agreement. We were both just really bad at our jobs. I always advocated for that, even now with my students. There's no reason to give your all to your nine-to-five. We walked to the waiting area and waited to be shuttled like everybody else onto the boat. I thought about running to someone who looked trustworthy and grabbing them by the arm and telling them everything: *I've been kidnapped!* But I started to trust him then. I still can't say why.

I was freezing, even with the heiress's coat. I handed him a Modelo, which he cracked open with a square thumb. There was a valley of veins moving over his hands, blue rivers poking underneath his hairless arms. I looked away when he lifted his scarf, which I felt him ask of me even though he hadn't opened his mouth.

"I feel like she actually would have loved all this," I said finally, breaking our contract. I sipped my beer. "She never gets out of that apartment, you know." He nodded, and I still didn't want to look at him. I could smell his sweat. It was the nervous kind, because of the consequences or because he was close to me. Some tourists were huddled in a small mass against the fence, taking photos of the Statue of Liberty. In a few years' time, I would go to Paris with a lover, one I'd meet at a farmers' market, overlapping my time with Lawrence. It would be dramatic and cause an entire friend group to never speak to me again. But we would go to Paris together and take the boat ride on the canal that takes you through the city. There I'd learn that the Eiffel Tower was built in two years and how, because of that, it needs to be repaired every six years, and the repairment itself always takes three. So many people get paid just to keep myths alive.

The Farmers' Market Guy and I would end things because he couldn't deal with my PTSD.

I looked toward my kidnapper, who had taken out his Android to snap a photo of the Statue of Liberty. Lighting up bits of the water, with the city twinkling behind her like millions of eyes, the statue was breathtaking. A teenager next to us held up a Bluetooth speaker blasting a New Order song. The air that was almost spring blew my hair back. How else can I tell you what I felt then? That the feeling, every so often, runs back to me like a dead family dog whenever I hear that song, whenever there's a body of water, whenever there's beer. I was alive, and that's all.

He pocketed his phone, looked at me, and shrugged. I laughed. I still wondered if I would die. If I would say, *But remember our moment?* as he pressed the gun to my temple. If I, with urine running down my leg, would plead, one last time, *Remember your phone and the statue and the teenager with the Bluetooth?* The ferry reached Staten Island too soon, and we both slowly made our way off. I was a little buzzed.

"Now we just go around and then back." I was excited to show him how simple it all was, how we could do it all over again if we wanted, going around like a record. It was a well-known hack. Something that was free, until they decided to take it away from us. We walked through the station, he and I, and stopped briefly at the gift store, and I thought of the Colombian heiress, looking for her name on the key chains but only finding mine. I couldn't buy anything. My wallet was in the backpack with the gun. He stood at the edge of the store, hands behind his back, like some kind of dad.

The call for the ferry came, and we sat inside this time. He cradled the backpack between his legs and dropped his head in his hands. I figured that if I was about to die, I might as well touch somebody, without force and full of intention and meaning. I remembered how Lawrence had a thing about elbows. How, when we would fuck, he'd pull my arms back and hold on to my elbows, not even looking at my face, just kissing them and nibbling on them a little bit. It really got him going. It also made me think about how underrated they are: pointy and fleshy, funny and there. I held on to my kidnapper's elbow like it was a handful of fruit or a doorknob, and he didn't shake me away or hold my elbow back. It was eighteen minutes of unconditional, one-way elbow holding, and I would keep doing this throughout my life, holding on to elbows when it mattered: Lawrence's again the night we got back together, my friend's during her last round of chemo, my mother's when I finally returned to the beautiful home I had run away from, the Farmers' Market lover's, my now ex-husband's, my son's.

The ferry pulled back into the Manhattan station. I told the kidnapper I had to pee. He waited by the entrance of the bathroom with my scab-colored backpack, and I held up two fingers. In the bathroom, I pissed out my beer, pulled up my cutoffs, tucked in my cotton T-shirt, and slipped on the heiress's coat again. I washed my hands and looked at myself in the mirror, pulled my hair back, then let it down again. I made faces in the mirror as if I were talking to him, seeing how I had looked, how I had behaved. When I opened the door, my backpack was on the floor, and he was gone.

I took the 4 and switched to the J at Fulton, looking around me and seeing only a police officer on his phone.

"Excuse me?" I said, trying to fill my mouth with saliva. He peered up at me, and I realized I didn't know what I would say. Would I change the color of the handkerchief of the kidnapper because I wanted to protect him? Had they already gone back for the Colombian heiress? Was it already too late? Would he come back for me?

"Ma'am?"

"Is this the right way to go downtown?" He pointed to a sign and grunted, then returned to his phone. On the train, I kept thinking I saw the kidnapper in every flash of yellow. When I got home and charged my phone, I messaged the Colombian heiress on WhatsApp.

Hey, are you okay?

Yes, she responded, too quickly. *Why?*

Nothing. Stay safe out there.

Gracias :] I loved the micheladas today!!!! I fell asleep and dreamed of lights behind cloth. I skipped my classes that week and saw nobody. I worked on some writing, but everything was too long and rambled, like I didn't really know what I wanted to say.

Finally, the following Thursday, I arrived at the Colombian heiress's apartment. Jorge opened the door. He told me she had left a week ago, and he could not tell me where, for security reasons.

I was sweating beneath my jean jacket. "If you hear from her," I asked him, "can you tell her to text me?" I didn't want to admit that I wished I could've said goodbye—and I still do, because I never saw her again. Her presence on socials was blank; a few fake ones popped up and then vanished. There was nothing reported on the news. When I called the embassy, they were tight-lipped, then asked me why I was so concerned.

"I will," Jorge said, and I swear to God, he winked at me, and then he closed the door.

I walked to where I had locked my bike, on some scaffolding on Sixth Avenue, fully expecting it to be gone and calculating how much I would have to put aside to buy a new one. But my bike was still there, the one I'd bought used a few years before, with the basket an ex of mine had lovingly screwed on. In six years, it would get lost to a flood in my building. I'd have to find a new job, of course. I'd have to go back to the tutoring agency to see if they could place me with somebody else. One way of making a living leads to another, until something evil with health insurance sticks, like a start-up or a finance bro who is willing to marry you. That's what I used to think, anyway. About all of it.

I am so far into the future now, but I still feel like I am there. Or maybe I can just see her so clearly: this skinny girl unlocking her bike. I love her, checking her breaks, squeezing the wheels, patting rainwater off her seat, turning the pedals with her finger, clipping her helmet over her head, mounting the bike swiftly. What a silly girl, what a way of life. She pedals up the Williamsburg Bridge and races the J as it buzzes by, ass up, thighs strong. The train is always faster than her, but it's fun, for a moment, to believe. The road's treacherous and full of cement trucks and e-bike deliverymen, people in SUVs who can't see her and don't give a damn, assholes just trying to get where they need to go. She rides past white bikes chained to fences decorated with flowers, thinking, *That could be me.* She has seven hundred proud dollars to her name. She has a single KIND bar rattling around in her backpack. She has time.

Pool House

My mom always had plenty to say about Patty, and her mother, Helen, did, too. They would talk about Patty as my mom did Helen's nails. Patty had a drug problem. Patty dated a man who was telling her bad things. Patty adopted a cat, and then the cat ran away. Patty had "bad energy." When I asked my mom what "bad energy" meant, she said, "It's something that never leaves you if you aren't careful."

I only ever really saw Patty twice. It should've been four, but the third time, she didn't show up, and the last time, well, I still can't be sure that was her.

THE FIRST TIME

I'll never forget it. She marched into the salon my mom worked in, two Starbucks lattes clutched in her hands. I was in the waiting chair, the symbols on the math homework in front of me dancing into one another. My mom's boss, a tall woman with shiny cheek-bones, didn't like it when I was around; she felt it was distracting to the other clients. But it was a weekend, and my mom wanted to keep an eye on me.

"Here, Helen," Patty said, handing her the latte. Helen was "Helen," not "Mom."

"Patty, have you met Claudia's daughter?"

Patty turned around and smiled at me with her blocky white teeth. I could see a film of spit on them. She stretched out her hand. She had chipped purple paint on her nails, like she didn't care about that sort of thing. She smelled like flowers trying to overpower cig-arettes trying to overpower flowers. She had a pointy nose that on the wrong face would look piglike, but on her face looked angular, drawn on by God. She was wearing these jeans that showed off her pancake belly and shapely hips. My body was still pea-shaped. Blobby. Sexless. I held on to her hand and felt a booger hanging between my nostril and lip. I couldn't get anything out of my mouth. My mom looked up from Helen's pudgy feet. Age spots prickled Helen's calves, spider veins wrapping up her thighs.

"Say hi," Helen said. Helen had thick silver hair that stopped at her neck.

"She's shy," my mom said. Patty retracted her hand. I'd missed my chance.

"That's okay. I hate talking to strangers, too. See you later, Helen. Bye, Claudia's daughter." The bell jingled as she pushed through the door.

THE SECOND TIME

On another Saturday at the salon, Helen asked me to go through her purse while her nails were drying. My mom was ringing someone up at the desk. "In the front pocket," she said, motioning with her chin, "there's a twenty-dollar bill. Give it to Patty?" she said, with a wink. "She's outside in her Jeep." I rummaged through her scaly bag, extracting the crisp twenty-dollar bill between two fingers. I took a deep breath, checked my nose for any boogers, and made my way to her.

"Whaddup, troublemaker!" she said to me. Her nails, now painted white, clicked against the car door. I don't know why she called me a troublemaker. Had I done something bad? Was she making fun of me because I was the exact opposite of a trou-blemaker? I presented her the twenty, my hand shaking.

"Oh my God, thank *fucking* God. I'm starving. I could eat a cow." She lit a cigarette. "You wanna come get subs with me?" But then her phone started to ring through her speakers, making the doors vibrate, tickling my body.

"I thought I told you to leave me alone," she said to whomever was calling her, so serious that I wasn't sure if she was joking. I turned around, making my way back to the salon, where Helen was talking about how Patty was really making some posi-tive changes.

"She's getting up earlier. She's almost exactly where I need her to be. Ow! Claudia, that hurt." My mom apologized and continued to pluck the cuticles from Helen's toes. They snowed onto the towel. I guess Helen was Mom's friend. Or they were friends who'd met while my mom had been painting her nails.

"I just don't know where I went wrong with her," Helen said as my mom delicately painted the red polish onto her toes, and she soaked her hands in paraffin. Her middle toe had a silver ring on it in the shape of a spider, its legs hugging her swollen flesh. "I gave her everything. Swimming lessons on Saturdays. All the right tutors. Everything. Now it's like I don't even matter." My mom nodded. "I know what you did differently, Claudia. I mean, look how good this one turned out." Helen took her hand out from the paraffin wax.

"I always love this part," Helen said to me and only me. It was like we were in our own world, like my mom couldn't hear, her brow furrowed as she painted the final layer onto her toes. She peeled the paraffin wax off her hand in slow motion. The paraffin had always reminded me of the skin of summer rolls, and before I'd known better, I thought you could eat it. And before that, I'd thought it was part of your own skin, that the wax heated you up so specifically, it stripped part of you away. For a moment, I forgot all I had learned and saw Helen's hand as something that had just been born again, crimson and fleshy, pulsing and alive, the old skin flecking off in thick wads. My mom has hands that look like a man's. That's mean, but it's true. Fat blue veins bulge from them, and it looks like somebody sliced her fingers from a block of clay. Her boss walked by. "Claudia, can I speak to you for a second?" I padded back to the waiting chair, trying to make myself invisible as the boss spoke to her without sound, smiling with her eyes narrowed, pretending like what she was saying was from a place of care.

THE THIRD TIME

"Why doesn't she hang out with Patty one of these days? Maybe tomorrow?" Helen asked my mom, handing her card over for her latest manicure. "Get her out of your hair. Patty needs somebody to be a role model to." She winked at me. "Really?" my mom said, handing her the receipt. "Are you sure?"

I was surprised my mom was okay with me hanging out with Patty for a day, but I think she didn't have a choice. I didn't want to be in the salon anymore. I wanted to be sitting in a car with Patty while she blasted music with swears. I wanted her to take out a packet of cigarettes from the glove compartment and say, *Don't tell the moms.* I wanted to sit at The Cheesecake Factory and order the Santa Fe salad. I wanted her to rub lipstick on our hands in neat lines of pink at Macy's. I wanted her to show me how to be.

So my mom and I drove over to Patty's place for our big day together. Patty lived in Helen's pool house. Helen had turned it into an apartment after Patty had decided not to go to college.

This way Patty got to live as her own woman without ever really having to move far away. It made me sad to think that Patty would ever even think to do that. It made me scared to think that I would want to, too.

"Call Patty," my mom told me, handing me her phone. "Tell her we're on our way." I took a deep breath and called. Her phone went immediately to voicemail. I called again. Nothing. We pulled up to the pool house and hopped out, the gravel popping underneath our shoes. The pool house had two floors and a garage and was painted a cream color on the outside. An off-white. My mom pronounced it "off-of-white." She knocked calmly on the door. Nobody came down. The glass window on the door was too high for me to see anything, so I jumped to get a better look. I thought I saw a blob of flesh and underwear, but when I jumped again, there was nothing and no one. My mom's knocking became more frantic. I imagined the door wincing every time her fist landed, big welts forming at its edges. "I'm going to be late," she said under her breath.

I snatched up a piece of gravel, aiming it at the glass window on the door. My mom grabbed my wrist. "This isn't your property," she said, sternly. I gave my face little exercises to keep from crying, the gravel falling back to the ground. My mom was never really one to explode, but her anger simmered, always threatening to boil over but never getting there. Like if I went to touch her, I'd burn myself. I waited for Patty to open the door in a swift, loving pull, to look me in the eyes and say, "Let's have some fun today, troublemaker." But after ten minutes of waiting and my mom's frantic banging, we climbed back into the Subaru and made our way to the salon.

There I took a seat once more in a waiting chair. I shook my sandaled foot up and down. My mom whispered something to her boss and pointed at me while shaking her head apologetically. Her boss nodded and said something back that I couldn't hear. I was worried my mom would be in trouble, but mostly I was sad about Patty. My butt grew sore from sitting. Disinfectant filled my nose. I kept looking at the glass door, thinking I'd hear it jingle to announce Patty coming for me. But every jingle was just another client and never Patty. I read the celebrity magazines front to back. An actress from a canceled show came home to a stalker sleeping in her bed. A British heartthrob was having an affair with his nanny. Everybody's secret lives. I wondered if I'd ever be famous and if anyone would ever write about how much weight I'd lost after having a baby. My mom was filling up the pedicure tub with bleach when Helen called.

"You know how she is," I heard Helen's voice say on speaker-phone. "She went out last night with that man again and didn't come back till later, then I guess she slept through all your calls and woke up at four a.m. I'm sorry, Claudia." The bleach bubbles popped; steam rose.

"Oh, Helen," she said, shutting the water off. "I understand. No worries." My mom hung up the phone and sighed. She looked at me and shrugged. In the car, she pinched the cross we had dangling in the Subaru. It twirled as we drove along, and I felt safe watching it dance as my mom's fingers absently moved, and I felt safe as she muttered to herself about things she needed to do later: pick up groceries, call the bank. I was in a trance of safety when my mom slammed on the brakes, cursing in Spanish, because there was a man standing in front of her Subaru.

He had a fluffy blond haircut parted in the middle, the strands of his bangs curtaining over his white sunglasses. He had the kind of hair I'd seen on television shows in the late afternoon, the sun aging beneath the drapes. His puffy pink lips parted into a grin, and for whatever reason, I knew that he was grinning at me. I felt disgusted and scared, but maybe that's the only way I knew how to describe it. My mom honked loudly, hitting the steering wheel with her big hands, her nostrils flaring. The man walked backward so that he was facing us, still grinning as he nearly danced on the whites of the crosswalk. He waved. "What is he, blind?" My mom threw up a veiny middle finger at him, and we sped away, the cross jerking around.

The next day, as a kind of apology, Helen came by our house to drop off a garbage bag full of Patty's clothes. She said Patty wanted me to have them. Helen had done this before—gifted me Patty's old things and told me it was because Patty had said so. I had a stack of Patty's books that felt like furniture in my room. This new bag was full of thin designer T-shirts and leather pants, fuzzy pink bucket hats with the price tags still on. There was even a half-empty bottle of pink perfume that said *yummy* on the front of it. "Try it on!" Helen insisted. "Go into the bathroom and do a fashion show!" In the bathroom, I slipped on a black shirt that had *bebe* bedazzled on it, cut for a woman's body, tight at the waist and looser at the breast and hip. It gave me hope to grow into. I lifted my arms in the mirror, and the shirt stayed in place. I twisted in it back and forth, imagining myself more like Patty: taller, blonder, booby-er, less hairy, with a face that was completely symmetrical. I felt a pinch on my stomach, which I was always sucking in because of that embarrassing pea shape, and saw a little spider there, silver and dangly. I slapped it and plucked its flattened corpse off with my finger. Outside our bathroom, my mom was cleaning cuticle cutters, and Helen was waiting for me, fingers clasped.

"Oh, don't you just look *adorable*!" Helen said. She took out a digital camera. "I have to take a photo and show Patty; she'll die." The camera clicked, and she giggled, crow's feet bunching up by her eyes. I smiled but only with my teeth, my lips flipping out like the lips of those animated cartoons made of clay that I hated.

"I don't like these clothes," my mom said later, chucking them all back into the garbage bag. "They have bad energy." I agreed, thinking of the spider. Still, I hid the *yummy* perfume bottle from her behind my Princess Diaries books, and I sprayed it on myself when I was alone with the door closed, smelling likes roses and champagne. I guess my mom found the perfume, because it disappeared from the hiding place the next day.

THE LAST TIME

"Maybe you can put this on your résumé," my mom said as we drove to Helen's house one last time. Helen had asked my mom if I would be interested in sorting through her papers for money. My mom was relieved that she could have somewhere to keep me for the day and comforted by the fact that I would be with an adult and not a flaky almost adult.

It was the middle of July, and the heat wasn't letting up. After we pulled into the driveway, the cross dangling and the gravel popping and the pool house looming before us, my mom squirted Banana Boat SPF 50 into my palm and had me rub it all over my exposed skin.

"But I thought I was going to be inside," I said. I could feel the SPF 50 leaking into my eyes and the corners of my mouth, probably making its way into my bloodstream and slowly poisoning me. I looked like a ghost.

"You never know," my mom said, snapping the bottle closed and burrowing it back into her purse. "Now you're protected." She kissed me on the forehead. "Remember to be polite," she said, "and *grateful* for the opportunity. And try not to talk to Patty. I don't like that girl." She honked the horn and blew me an absent-minded kiss as she pulled away. I walked down a path lined with tall bushes. The gravel beneath my sandals was white as bone, and I pictured them crunching little skeletons. I found myself at a pair of tall bushes standing guard over Helen's pool, where Helen was sitting on a lawn chair in a simple blue one-piece bathing suit. I don't know how else to say this: Helen looked younger.

My mom looked younger than she really was, so I always assumed people were older. Helen was always asking my mom what her secret was, and my mom would say something about some cream the salon was selling. The Helen before me wasn't someone who needed creams. She had the body of a teenager, with a round, lumpless butt and boobs that sat high beneath her swimsuit. Her arms were the color of honey and no longer speckled with spots. Her silver hair was now platinum blonde.

"There's my girl!" she said, her young arms open. I accepted her embrace. Her armpit sweat left a damp trail on me.

"Pool looks nice, right? Hey, anytime you want to come over and just go for a dip, you let me know. Take off your shoes, make yourself at home!"

"Thank you," I said, slipping off my sandals and dipping my feet into the pool. "It looks nice."

"I really want to host more parties here. When's your birthday? Have it here! Wouldn't that be fun? A pool party. You could invite all your friends!" I thought about the people I could invite. Christie had moved away. My mom might be working. Maybe Patty would be around. Helen's phone dinged.

"Actually, this is one of my friends. They're coming over later. You'll meet them."

"Okay," I said. The lower halves of my legs were starting to change color.

"Look at that," Helen said, brushing her hand against my leg. Her hand was smaller than it was when it was in the paraffin, less knuckly, with sharp green nails at the end. My mom must've done them. "You're so lucky. I just burn right up."

"Thank you," I said.

"I'd kill for your skin. Honest to God, I would."

A noise came from the pool house that made me jump. It sounded like a door opening, a big, creaking kind of thing, but when I looked, the door to the pool house was shut. I shook my leg up and down. I looked around us. Just tall bushes and the pool and the pool house at the far end, sitting there like an off-white box. Helen didn't seem to hear it, because she was still talking. "I need to set better intentions next cycle," Helen said. "I don't always get it right."

"Is Patty home?" I said, interrupting her, my foot dipping in and out of the pool. Helen scratched the space behind her sunglasses and shrugged. She seemed to be looking at something but not the pool house. She looked past her sliding doors, into her kitchen. She took off her sunglasses and blinked. I don't like how sometimes people's eyes look so much tinier when they take off their glasses. Her mouth opened slightly, the way a cat's does after she's finished giving herself a bath. There were no lines around her mouth. No crow's feet by her eyes.

"Oh," I said, "is Patty inside?"

She didn't answer me and put her sunglasses back on. Whenever people don't answer me after I've asked a question, I never know if I should've asked it louder or if I should've just shut up in the first place. Maybe I was being annoying. Maybe I should've been minding my own business. I decided to let it go and watched my reflection in the dark frames of her glasses. I turned my head back and forth like I was listening to a song, watched my two heads in the lenses do the same. Helen flashed me a smile.

"Let's get started on this job I have for you, huh? You're really the perfect person for it."

The central AC greeted us with a thick chill. Everything was all blue on the inside. Everywhere a pale, approachable blue. I rubbed my arms.

"I have a sweater if you want one," she said. "What size are you? What are you, ninety-five pounds soaking wet?"

"A hundred seven pounds," I said. "And no thank you." I didn't want my mom to drive up and see me wrapped in someone else's sweater and yell at me again about bad energy, which is something I still didn't really understand. But it was Patty's energy that was bad, anyway, not Helen's. Helen's kitchen had an island and white lights reaching down from the ceiling. Helen and Patty smiled at me from frames above the stove, a silver wire connecting them to each other. There were no photos of Patty younger than my age, and no photos of Patty's father.

Helen led me to her office with a towel wrapped around her waist so she wouldn't drip on the lush carpet. There were photos all over the walls, with frames that were made of mirror. Here was young Helen skiing, though maybe it was this Helen, the one I knew. Young Helen in front of a brand-new car. Above the desk, there was a big mirror that was framed by more mirror and two windows. Walking past it, I saw something following me, but I realized it was just an illusion. A mirror on top of another mirror, making a joke.

"I've been meaning to sort through these for forever," Helen said, lifting different colored files from various gray cabinets and setting them on the floor for me, "but you know how it goes."

"What are they, exactly?" I asked.

"Just a few things I need to put in order," she said, looking at me blankly. "Arrange them in whatever way makes the most sense." She was standing over me with her manicured hands on her toweled hips, her sunglasses still on. Her toenails were bright red and shiny. My mom must've done those, too. "Does a hundred dollars sound good for the whole day?" I nodded. Was I supposed to negotiate? She laughed to herself. "Maybe we should've signed a contract or something. I'll be out by the pool if you need anything. Don't be shy." Then she slinked away from me, her back limber and strong, her hand clutching the towel around her waist, the carpet absorbing all her noise.

I sat on my hands for a while because it was so cold. I pulled two files out and set them in front of me. How was I supposed to know how to organize them if I didn't know what was in front of me? Opening the file, I felt a pinch on my finger, and all these spiders danced out, silver and dangly like the one that bit me from the *bebe* shirt. I shoved the papers away, then tried to kill all the spiders with the other file. I saw their bodies smoosh, and I shook their corpses into a small metal garbage can. Outside Helen was talking on the phone and laughing. The bushes rustled, and I thought I saw a hand peek out of one, but I knew I was just uncomfortable and seeing things. I decided not to organize the files by anything but color, but then a page slipped out, and I saw Patty's photo. She was my age here. The page read:

Girl, 12, 90 lbs.

That was the only thing on the page. I slid out another page with my finger. Another photo of a girl, but I didn't recognize her. She was in a bathing suit and not looking at the camera.

Girl, 12, 89 lbs.

I shut the files. They felt dirty. For some reason, I thought of the man in front of the car and how I'd felt when he'd looked at me. Was I sick in some way? I placed the files in a pile that I decided would be the red pile, because I didn't know what I was doing, really.

My fingers were dry and stiff from the AC. The hairs on my arms were standing up like a caterpillar's. I tucked my arms into my T-shirt. My stomach whispered at me. I needed to take a break. Maybe I would feel better if I just got something to eat. Helen would understand. I lifted myself up from the mess I'd made and walked across the lush carpet and back outside.

"Hey, little thing!" Helen said, looking up from her book. "You working hard in there?" She looked at me from underneath her sunglasses.

"Yeah!" My voice was high.

"I knew you'd be perfect for it," she said. I didn't really think about what that meant, because I was too distracted by how good it felt to be outside. The sun coating me in warmth. The tip of my nose relaxing.

"Are you hungry?"

I pinched my elbows and nodded.

"I'm starving." She held out her phone. Adults were always giving me their phones. "Do me a favor. There's a number on the fridge; order us some subs."

I thanked her and took the phone, imagining what would happen if my fingers lost their grip and I dropped it into the pool. Or if I threw it into the pool on purpose. Or if I put it in my mouth and then swallowed it. These thoughts followed me to the fridge, where nothing was held together by a magnet. It was a stainless steel I could nearly see myself in. I thought that maybe this was a test, so I opened the fridge, and . . . there was nothing. No eggs and no bread, no mayonnaise, no cheese, no meat. Nothing but the medical lights of a fridge's insides. Clutching Helen's phone, I walked back outside, but Helen wasn't there. A gust of hot wind swept by, rustling the pages of her book.

"Helen?" Her phone buzzed in my hands. It was an unknown number. I didn't know if it was bad to answer, if I would get in trouble. It kept buzzing. "Hello?" No answer. I hung up. The phone buzzed again. I made it go to voicemail. I sat down in Helen's green pool chair and waited. Where could she have gone? The bushes around the pool swayed in the breeze. I picked up Helen's book. When I opened it, I braced myself for spiders, but none came out. The book, like the fridge, was empty. Had she been writing in a journal? I went to the first page, which you're never supposed to write on because of bad luck, and there was a photo of me in Patty's clothes, and underneath my photo, in scrawling letters, it said: *Girl, 12, 107 lbs. That's strange*, I thought. *I don't like that.* That feeling again. Sweat dripped down the back of my neck. The skin on my calves was turning a dark, wooden color. I ran to the sliding screen doors to relieve myself from the heat, but they were locked. I jumped from one foot to the other, the concrete searing my heels. I felt like a little animal. I felt smaller than I ever had before. I took off my shirt and my knee-length shorts, plugged my nose, and jumped into the pool. Sweet release. Popping out of the water and gasping for air, I opened my eyes and saw a man standing at the edge of the pool. But when I wiped the water out of my eyes, he was gone.

I crouched back into the water, dipping half my face into the pool, turning around in a circle like an alligator, like a hunting thing. A cloud of red stretched from me as I turned. I stood up. The red spread and spread. I covered my face, but the cloud just kept growing, the blood mixing with the Banana Boat sunscreen. The last time I'd had a nosebleed like this was a few months ago, in my sleep. I'd woken up, and my whole pillow had been soaked in my blood. I was almost proud of how much blood I had inside me, how much of it had been ready to escape.

I wiped my nose across my arm. I lifted myself out of the pool and tried to find my shirt. Where was my shirt? I covered my nose with one hand and the hair peeking from my underwear with the other. Helen's phone was right where I'd left it, but my clothes were gone. I told myself not to jump to conclusions: Helen was trying to kill me, the pool was something that'd suck me up if I didn't get out in time, she was writing a recipe in her notebook to cook me.

I convinced myself that Helen would show up, and I'd tell her about jumping to conclusions. "That's quite an imagination you have! You're so scared," she would say, "because you are so smart!"

I sat again in the pool chair, my knees bunched to my chest, trying to feel so smart. I thought of calming things. Making an *X* with a glue stick on a piece of paper. The sound ice makes in a cold glass of water. Mom talking on the phone as I fell asleep. How sometimes, in the middle of a sentence, she'd trail off, and her voice would stretch from her in a funny croak, and how I was the only one who ever really heard it, so I couldn't be sure if I was making that sound up or not.

"Whaddup, troublemaker! I didn't know you were here!"

I turned, and there she was: Patty. Her head was sticking out of the pool house window like a daisy. Her long honey hair hanging still in the hot air. Her burnt-syrup skin, her symmetrical face. I couldn't see her features from where I was. I squinted to see her better. Mom said that she would get skin damage from all that time spent in tanning booths, that her skin would fall from her in wrinkly sheets when she got older. But I thought that she looked nice. Plus she remembered me.

"Oh my God, are you bleeding? Where are your clothes, silly? Come up here. There's AC!"

She ducked her daisy head back inside. The door to the pool house was open. Had I missed her opening it? Maybe that's where Helen had gone. All I knew was that I didn't want to stay outside, seminaked by the pool, where the man potentially was. I grabbed Helen's phone and hopped up the driveway, wincing as my feet kissed the hot gravel. There was a welcome mat that said *COME IN*, so I did. I stepped inside, trying to shake off the water without getting blood everywhere. The AC felt amazing, but to be honest with you, the place was gross. Patty's shirts were in clumped piles all over the floor. Candy wrappers glimmered, bottles of lotion lay on their sides, cardboard boxes stacked in a shifty tower. The light from the oven was glowing, and it was turned up to 350 degrees. I heard rap music blasting from upstairs.

I stepped over the bottles and the candy wrappers and stood before the staircase, where there was another mirror lined with mirror. I saw myself, this stupid girl in a wet training bra and too-big underwear bunched up at the ass, hair sprouting from her bikini line.

I followed the rap music, wondering if it ever scared Patty to keep music on so loud. What if somebody came and she couldn't hear it? My nose was still bleeding. There were streaks from it on both my arms and little droplets of sunscreen moving down them like paint. I reached the room with the rap music and knocked. No answer. I tried the handle. It opened.

In Patty's room, the day moved five hours ahead. Black curtains, black dressers. More shirts on the floor. Trash bags, probably full of more clothes. Cigarette butts in a wineglass. The same bottle of *yummy* perfume her mom had given me on a dresser. All of Patty's things but no Patty. I pulled a *bebe* shirt from the floor that looked just like the one that had been in the garbage bag of bad energy. Was it the same one? It couldn't have been. I found a pair of athletic shorts in a pile and pulled them over my two-toned legs. Patty wouldn't mind. I sprayed myself with the *yummy* perfume and felt a little better. I had even stopped bleeding. I found a phone plugged into a speaker and pressed pause to hear myself think.

But then a loud ring made the room shiver. I covered my ears like a spoiled kid in a corner of a party who wants to go home.

But that was me: I didn't like this party, and I wanted to leave. I unplugged Patty's phone. An unknown number. I answered.

"Do you think you're perfect for it?" A man. His voice deep and confident but still boyish. I felt like I was going to have diarrhea all over Patty's floor. Somehow, with the phone against my ear, I pictured the man on the crosswalk. I could see him smiling into the receiver and feel the tickle of his blond hair against my cheek. Could he hear me breathing faster? Was he out there by the pool, there but not there?

"Do you want to stay for a while?"

I bit some dry skin off my lip and swallowed it. Maybe this was the time to say something funny, a joke that would fix all of this. *Knock knock, poop's there.* But no words came. Just my sharp breaths.

"Do you like the clothes you're wearing?"

I hung up and flung the phone onto the bed. I opened and closed my fists. How had he known what I was wearing? I looked around me. Was he here? I was really worried I would poop these athletic shorts. The room grew darker, but maybe that was just how it felt. Maybe this was a prank. Maybe Patty was sitting right next to that man. Maybe they were boyfriend-girlfriend, and she was telling the one she loved to tell me funny things.

"Patty?" I said, but part of me already knew it was useless. I sat on her bed. Patty's covers were made of soft white tuft-like material. I sank my hand into them. I noticed two pink openings. A tail. My hand was touching a fluffy white cat with a collar around her neck that read *Little Bitch*. She blended in with the covers. I made kissing noises at Little Bitch. I said, "Hello, beautiful girl. Hello, beautiful baby." I petted her neck, scratched behind her ears. She didn't respond. Her mouth was slightly open, revealing tiny white teeth. I looked closer. There were empty red sockets where her eyes should have been. Her stomach didn't rise or fall. Little silver spiders were crawling out of her open mouth one by one. I leaped from the bed as more and more marched out. There must have been hundreds of them. They changed the color of the bed with their wriggling bodies. The phone rang again, but I didn't dare answer.

Somebody was knocking on the door downstairs. *Okay*, I thought to myself. Maybe Patty got locked out. Maybe Patty was just really messy, the kind of girl who never swept under her bed or noticed her cat died. The knock was polite at first and then shifted to pounding. Maybe this was an emergency, and Patty needed me. Maybe I could save her. I tiptoed down the stairs, making them creak. A blob bounced up to the window of the door, casting a shadow over the staircase like a hand over a flashlight. I twisted the doorknob and pulled. It wouldn't open. The pounding continued. "I'm going to be late," I heard my mother say. Pound, pound, pound.

"Mom!" I yelled, pounding back and yanking at the doorknob. "Mami, it's me! Something's wrong!" I cried and screamed for her. She didn't hear me. She pounded, and I pounded back. I heard two pairs of feet make their way across the gravel. A car door opened and then slammed closed. The engine faded as our Subaru drove farther and farther away. I wiped my snot on my *bebe* shirt. Patty's *bebe* shirt.

I climbed back upstairs, snot still swinging from my nose. There were spiders everywhere. The room was shimmering with them. I placed Helen's phone next to Patty's, and they started ringing at the same time, vibrating against each other as they were engulfed by spiders. I backed away from them.

"They'll take you," I heard Patty's voice say from the cat's pink parted mouth. "You're lucky it was so hot today." What did she mean? I looked down at my bloody, sunscreened arms. Bad energy. I ripped off Patty's clothes, and I bolted out of the room, nearly naked again, almost tripping down the stairs. I twisted the knob and pushed the door again, and this time it gave way. And there, at the end of the driveway, was the man with the fluffy haircut and white sunglasses. My hand was so small and useless gripping the doorknob.

"Who are you?" I asked. I couldn't make out his face, but I saw those puffy lips that had made me uneasy. He moved a step forward.

"Where's Helen?" I asked him. "Where's Patty?" He took another step forward. He lifted his sunglasses up and squinted at me.

"She gets like this," the man said, grinning.

"Who are you?" I clenched the doorknob harder. He shifted his sunglasses back onto his nose and stood there with his hands in his pockets. He was patient and smiling at me with all his teeth, like he knew everything that could ever happen to me.

"You can't come with me," the man said. "Not yet." A spider walked up my leg. I slapped it dead. I turned around and saw spiders spilling from the doorframe, ready to consume me. When I turned back, the man was gone. I ran over the scorching gravel. I ran past another beautiful house and then another, took a left turn, and kept running. I didn't know where I was going or what had happened to Patty, but I knew that my mom was somewhere and that she could cover my body and take me inside, where it was cooler, where it was safe. I knew that one day, the protection would run out, and I'd have to figure it out myself or protect somebody else. Until then, I ran, and when the skin on my heels blistered and broke, I ran on my toes, like I do in my dreams, like I don't weigh anything at all.

Tails

I never thought I'd have to make the choice, but you're never prepared until you have to be. It happened after my stepaunt came to visit me at work. She's my stepaunt because she's the aunt after my uncle divorced my real aunt, though I guess I also wasn't related to that aunt to begin with. I work at a hospital as a hospital waitress. We wear white button-downs and black bow ties, black aprons. Sometimes the neck of the white button-down will get all yellow if you don't do a good-enough job of cleaning it, but that never happens to me. I'm meticulous about that kind of thing. I had my fresh uniform on when I arrived at Bariatric Surgery with my rolling cart of food. I slid out a gray tray with a maroon top, which carried red Jell-O and apple juice inside.

"Beatrice?" I said, reading from the white slip. I looked up, and there she was, my stepaunt Beatrice, grinning with a manicured hand over her stomach.

"Oh," I said. "It's you. Is everything okay?"

"I swallowed a pin."

"How'd that happen?"

"Long story, hun. And we don't have a lot of time. Shut the door." I did as she said, even though you're not technically allowed to be in the room alone with the patient.

"I have an opportunity for you, and since I have no heirs—"

"Heirs?"

"Yes, you know how the queen had Prince Charles?"

"Right."

"And Prince Charles has Prince William, who has Prince George?"

"Yes."

"Well, I have nobody. And you are my closest of kin."

I was flattered by that—I always thought my stepaunt was cool. She was from Dubai and had the best fashion. I loved her intricate scarves and flowing pants, her full-throttle laugh that sounded like she was chugging sunlight. But right now, she was confusing me. She took out a vial that held a dark worm in blue liquid.

"What is that?"

"This was meant for you. I've been holding on to it for you."

"Is it alive?"

"Liz, you're hairy." I thought back to a moment when a boy I had liked in middle school said that he thought my legs looked just like the gym teacher's. I had been considering getting all of it lasered once I had the funds.

"I mean, yeah, but I take care of it." I had an at-home wax kit, tweezers. There were little pimples from ingrown hairs exploding under my chin and on my bikini line. And sometimes, especially in the hospital lights, it looked like I had a five-o'clock shadow.

"This can fix everything for you." I was self-conscious because no one had mentioned I was hairy; I just thought it was something I was overly concerned about. But here she was, confirming the ingrown hairs, the five-o'clock shadow.

"What does it do?"

"You attach it to the end of your backbone. Then all the hair that you ever had on your body will take the form of a tail."

"Excuse me?"

"Yes," she said. "You heard me right." Her eyes were wide. "And if you don't choose the tail, you'll have the opposite of the tail."

"Which is what?"

"Completely hairy all over. A beast, basically."

"Why would I want that? Does the tail grow?"

"Elizabeth, do you want to participate in your heritage, or do you want to let it die?"

"Well, it's not really my heritage," I said, wondering why she was being so insistent. "I only met you last year."

"Look at the hair. See how it points toward you?" The hair floated in the tube of blue liquid. To me it didn't seem like it was pointing any which way. Somebody knocked on the door.

"Hello!" It was the nurse. "Have you peed yet?"

"*HOLD ON A FUCKING SECOND!*" my stepaunt screamed. Then she looked back at me and returned to her calm yet insistent demeanor. "It's meant for you."

"Did you swallow a pin on purpose?" I didn't understand what was going on. "Why didn't you just call me if you wanted me to do this?"

"It was a matter of urgency. Also, it's already been decided. If you don't do this, the tradition will die, and in many ways, we will all die, too. And you can always give it to somebody else. If it doesn't suit you. Did I mention that?"

"No," I said, "you didn't. But all right, sure." I took the vial and dropped it in my apron to make her happy. She was probably still high from the anesthesia. Tears welled in my aunt's eyes, and I couldn't tell if they were happy tears, like she was watching a movie about somebody overcoming inconceivable odds, or tears of relief, like she just found out she wasn't pregnant.

"Wonderful," she said. "Amazing. Thank you, Liz."

"Sure," I said, genuinely worried about my aunt's mental health. I opened the door for the nurse, who was holding a plastic tube for my aunt, presumably for her to piss in. I pushed the cart of food—the chicken cutlets for the maternity ward, the

Styrofoam cups of ice cream for the children's ward, the chocolate pudding with the plastic spoons for the psych ward—out of the way and into the hallway, where people were visiting their loved ones and doctors were delivering the good news or the bad news.

I punched out of my shift and changed back into my normal clothes. I took the vial out of my apron and got a good look at it. I figured the blue liquid must be keeping the hair intact. I nestled the vial into the pocket of my jeans. I said goodbye to the head chef, who I hated. He was always talking about how he was gonna name his first daughter Lorna Doone, like after the cookies. How did he know what she wanted to be named? I waited for the train underneath a heat lamp next to an advertisement about health insurance, which I was thankful I didn't need because of the hospital. It was cold that day. My coworker Montgomery waited with me.

"How are you today, Liz?" he asked me from underneath his puffy jacket.

"Kind of weird day. How are you?"

"I am blessed!" Montgomery said, which he always did. He was old and from Haiti and had been doing this job forever. He always tricked people into asking how they were so he could say, "I am blessed!" It felt like a gotcha moment. Like, *Oh, your day was fine? Well, mine, as always, was blessed, and also I pray to God, who hates you.*

"My stepaunt came to visit me today."

"Oh, and how is her health?"

"She was passing something down to me."

Montgomery got very serious. "She has passed on?" he said, holding a sleeve of his puffy jacket out to me. I touched his sleeve with mine like we were clinking a glass.

"No. Just, like, a family heirloom, I guess."

"Family is very important," Montgomery said. "It is the only thing in the world."

Montgomery was traditional and annoying but kind of in the way my parents are, because they're also immigrants. But he was never upset or mean to me about it, so I was never upset or mean to him back, even when he was spouting crap like "Family is very important. It is the only thing in the world" at me. I fingered the vial in my pocket and thought about heritage and that day in fourth grade when we all took a field trip to Ellis Island to find our ancestors, and I couldn't find mine because my ancestors were just my parents, who had only come here to this land ten years before.

I got off the train at Brighton Center and walked up the hill to Taco Wendy to treat myself to a Mexican hot chocolate. I always dumped the hot chocolate out after I ordered it because I was allergic to chocolate and all milks. It was just nice to smell. I knew that was a waste, but I always recycled the plastic lid from the cup, always. The paper cup wasn't actually recyclable because it was lined with wax. Not a lot of people know that. Lucas, the guy who worked the counter at Taco Wendy, and I had an agreement. He knew that I did this. He saw me do this a few times, but he never said anything. Just walked by, smiling with his thumbs up. It was our end-of-the-day tradition.

"Hi, Liz!" It was also always nice to see Lucas because of his smile. He had no hair on his face at all, because he's half-Japanese or something. I could probably grow a beard faster than him.

"Hi."

"How was your day?"

"Weird. My aunt visited me at work and gave me this vial of hair?"

"Family is so random!"

"Definitely. How was your day?"

"Someone went into the bathroom and put blue paint all over the walls!"

"Is that a euphemism for 'shitting all over the walls'?"

"No, it really was blue paint. They left the can in a corner!"

"Oh. Are you gonna wash it off?"

"I already did, which is too bad. I thought it looked kind of nice! Artsy. Hot chocolate?"

"Yes, please."

He turned around and added the special powder to the paper cup that wasn't recyclable and steamed the milk, which was soy because I told him I was lactose intolerant, even though I'm allergic to all nuts and soy. I don't even want to try oat milk. I watched one of his coworkers, a girl with dark hair and dark eyebrows, place her hands over his eyes.

"Guess who?"

"It's Whoolia!" he said, laughing the way he did, like somebody who knew him well was tickling him, with his eyes all scrunched up and his mouth smiling. He turned around. They were laughing with each other, which was worse than seeing them kiss, in my opinion. Lucas seemed to remember I was standing there, because he looked self-conscious.

"Oh, Liz! This is Julia." He smiled at me and at Julia, all nice and welcoming, like me and this Whoolia would go get our nails done together or whatever friends who are girls do.

"Hi."

"I've heard a lot about you, Liz. Dr. Liz!"

"I'm not a doctor," I said, taking out my faded wallet. "I'm a hospital food service worker. I serve people food who are in the hospital. The doctors don't even eat the food. They don't like it. It's the same food that they use for prisons." Julia did a little laugh to be polite. I am not a good person to make small talk with. I'm always saying stuff about prisons. Lucas handed me my hot chocolate, and it was warm beneath my palm, like I was holding his.

"Always good to see ya, dude! Ha-ha," he said, eyes scrunching up again. "Take care!" I sniffed the hot chocolate that Lucas made for me. Sometimes it hurt my feelings that he was so nice, because it didn't feel like it was special and just for me. The chocolate smell was so deep and rich and full, I wanted to cry. I wished I could sip it without my throat closing up and me collapsing on the tile floor, writhing and gasping for air among the stray tortilla chips, Lucas calling 911 but it being too late because I had expired, drool leaking from my mouth.

"You too," I said, "dude."

At home I hung up my puffy jacket and threw down my bag. I squirted soap onto my hands and carefully washed them for twenty seconds, making sure to get in between each finger crevice and scratching each palm to get underneath my fingernails. I took out a frozen bag of fries and chicken fingers and tossed them onto a tray, setting the oven to 375 degrees. While waiting, I took the vial out once again and thought about how weird my stepaunt Beatrice was. The only time I'd really talked to her was after my uncle had left my aunt. He had brought Beatrice over to Thanksgiving dinner, and everyone was trying very hard not to be scandalized. I asked her questions about her life, and she touched my hand a lot, smiling. She was the kind of person whose touch you felt on the backs of your ears, no matter where she touched you. I wondered, actually, if she were some kind of witch. I didn't know what was up with her. I was worried she was having a psychotic break, or if I was.

I opened the vial, and the hair bounced out of it. I got on my hands and knees, searching the tile floor for the hair, but it had already disappeared or blended in. It had become half of half of half of something. Like a cut-up piece of cilantro that's so tiny, it's actually an atom. *Whatever*, I thought, *it's gone.* The alarm dinged, and my smiley-face chicken fingers and fries were ready. I dipped them into ketchup. They weren't delicious, but they were familiar and they filled me up every day. How many people could say the same? They were also the only thing I could really eat without having an allergic reaction. I watched the news briefly and then turned it off. I boiled some hot water and I drank it, because it's good for digestion. I turned off all my lights. I thought about all the inside jokes Lucas and Whoolia must have had, because they circulated the same space every day. Inside jokes that started to lose the ends of their sentences, started becoming just one word that made you keel over, crack up. Words like "mop" or "au lait." I had no words people shared with me. Except for "blessed" with Montgomery.

I've had a few boyfriends and one girlfriend. I've had good sex, or at least sex that felt like it'd gone through its full circle: finished, complete, that was nice, can you leave my house now? People have liked some things about me, but then they all realized that I'm really boring because of my allergies and my dedication to my job. So it's been better this way, being alone.

———

It came to me the next morning in the shower, suddenly and certain of itself. The fancy shampoo for curly hair I spent money on fell off the shower shelf and onto the floor. I bent over to pick it up, and then the fancy conditioner I spent money on fell, too. Something was knocking it over. I looked up, and there it was, next to the showerhead: dark, spindly, and pincerlike. I screamed, and the tail started thrashing even more. I didn't know where it was coming from. I thought that maybe a racoon or mutant rat had broken in. I turned, and nothing. I looked up, and nothing. Finally I remembered my stepaunt and touched the space right above my butt crack. It was seamless; there wasn't even a rupture of skin. The skin became tail, and the tail became skin. I got out of the shower and looked in the mirror. Behind me there was the tail, about three feet long and high. I reached up to touch it. It was bristly, like if all the hair that had ever got caught in your drain hardened over time and maybe you stuffed it through a long cylinder tube. All my body hair was also gone. My legs, my groin, my armpits, my neck: I was as smooth as a seal. I honestly had never looked more radiant.

I called my stepaunt immediately, a towel covering me up and the tail sticking through it. She didn't answer. I gave myself a few minutes to cry, mourning my old tailless life. *I should've gone on more dates. I should've bought a one-way ticket to Greece and seen those old statues on that old island.* I noticed that the tail had stopped its incessant thumping and relaxed around me. It was as if it was responding to me and my tears. Then I tried something. I played one of my favorite songs, "Touch the Sky" by Kanye West. I don't know. It just makes me feel happy. You can hear it anywhere and feel like you're in the middle of a montage in a movie before things get too complicated. The trumpets came in and the drums too, and Kanye rapping, and I felt the tail shiver, as if it had just been stung by many bees. It vibrated, and the vibration turned into a wild thump. It could keep the beat. I walked around the apartment, and I clapped my hands, and I felt like the tail and I were RAs getting everybody excited about orientation. I watched the tail slice into pillows I had just purchased from Target. There was cotton everywhere. I found myself laughing. The tail whipped around. It pricked me on my arm.

"Okay, chill out." Then I turned on one of the saddest songs I've ever known, "Someday You'll Want Me to Want You" by Brenda Lee, which I've maybe listened to after I throw out the hot chocolates that Lucas gave me. The tail shivered again and fell limp to the ground. I gathered it and fit it around me like a scarf.

I brushed my hand against the tail. I decided, as you often do in your life, to get used to this. I adjusted my clothes, cutting holes two inches wide in all my pants and skirts. I fit the tail through one of the holes and then wrapped it around my neck. It was still sleeping. I called out sick and decided to go to the library to do some research on women and tails. But before that, I made my way to Taco Wendy. I slowly walked down the hill and took deep breaths, keeping the tail cool. I held on to it and stroked it softly, like it was an unruly cat. Had I grown protective of it already? As I reached Taco Wendy, I felt the tail stir.

I stood in line and saw Lucas ringing people up for breakfast burritos. The tail stiffened around me, choking me like a snake squeezing its prey. I began losing air. I unwrapped it from my neck, and the tail started knocking bottles of hot sauce off the shelves; shirts that said *TACO WENDY!* on them collapsed to the ground. I went to gather them, flushed, completely embarrassed. The tail swiped the pieces across the floor.

"Ow!" I heard a woman say, her hand over her arm, where she was bleeding. "What the fuck?!"

Lucas was on the floor with me, gathering up the mess. "Liz!" he said. "Everything okay?!"

"Yeah, I just—I got a new pet."

"I don't think we allow snakes in the restaurant. Unless they're a support animal!" I could tell it hurt him to say something confrontational, which annoyed me. "And I would also have to see proper documentation if that's the case. Or some sort of vest!"

"Right. Well, I better go. Sorry, Lucas." I left Taco Wendy with little tears brimming in my eyes, wondering what kind of snake, exactly, wears a vest. Of course, as soon as I started crying, the tail relaxed and went limp again. I wrapped it around me and walked to the library. I held on to the tail the way you hold on to your braids when you're thinking or your backpack when you're running late for class. I tried to call my stepaunt, but the call went straight to voicemail.

At the library, I searched for "women and tails" and sorted through a shitboat of information: interspecies relationships, mermaids, selkies. Then I looked up "vestigial tails," because that's what this was: an organ like a tonsil or an appendix, something that I'd evolved past but still somehow carried with me, though it was really not my choice to.

VESTIGIAL TAILS: A STUDY, AN ANOMALY, A LIFE BY GERTRUDE LYPEPHORN

Coming from the French word "vestige," meaning "footprint" or "trace," vestigial organs are an evolutionary curiosity. For reasons unknown, we still have tonsils and appendixes, and some of us even have tails.

She went on to talk about people who lived with tails and even showed some gruesome photos of tails poking out of people's ass cheeks. I was thankful that my tail looked pretty, at least. Shapely. The same dark color as my hair. When I brushed it the opposite way, the hair felt curly. I wondered if I could dig all the way to the bone. I tried to find Gertrude's information, but she had died just two years ago. I wanted to cry. I didn't know who could help me with this. I found myself in a rideshare with the windows down, asking the driver to please play "Skinny Love" by Bon Iver on a loop, while the tail rested mournfully around my neck.

I thought about the choices that were in front of me, all of which felt like old bananas in Ziploc bags. Who would ever want that? Either I find somebody to bestow the tail on to or give up the tail and be covered in fur. That's what she said, wasn't it? I hated living a life with these choices. I didn't know why it was supposed to be this complicated. I decided to go the liquor store because I deserved a drink. In the whiskey aisle, I found Lucas, leaned over, talking to a cat.

"What is your name, buddy?" he was saying to the cat. "What have you seen in this world?" The cat blinked at him. I watched his fingers gently tickle her fur and heard the cat purr. My heart raced, and the tail tightened around my neck.

"Fuck." I thought I said it under my breath, but he heard me.

"Dr. Liz!" he said, eyes all scrunched up. "Did you know there was a cat here?"

"No," I said, trying to envision all my loved ones covered head to toe with leprosy and not Lucas's gentle hands petting gentle animals. He stood up, and his face got all serious. He had deep smile lines.

"Hey, I'm sorry if it felt like I was kicking you out earlier. I wasn't."

"That's okay," I said, grabbing the first bottle of whiskey I could find.

"I was just thinking out loud, which I do sometimes when I get nervous. Julia always says that I do that!" I was starting to lose circulation in my neck. I thought of dead baby birds on the cement in the beginning of spring.

"You look kind of different," he said. "Shiny!"

"New routine," I said. I cleared my throat. "I'll see you around." I turned around, hating myself.

"Liz!" I heard him say behind me. "A group of us are going to the movies tomorrow to see an old movie! I was wondering if maybe you wanted to come?" I gripped the whiskey bottle. I wanted to chug it all the way down. I could be calm. I could be normal.

"Yeah," I said. "Sounds fun."

"Cool!" he said, stuffing his hands in his pockets like a cowboy. "Well, I'll see you there! Coolidge Corner Theatre! Eight p.m.!" I nodded and almost sprinted to the checkout counter. I practically slipped on the ice in front of my house; I was running away from my feelings so hard. I took off my jacket, and the tail unfurled, sitting stiff and upright next to me. A complete horndog. I uncapped the whiskey and took a swig. The tail slowly deflated, and I wondered about how in the hell I was supposed to live the rest of my life.

Passing by a sushi restaurant on my way to the movies, I saw my stepaunt Beatrice laughing freely with a man who had chopsticks in his mouth and was pretending to be a walrus. When she saw me, she stood up, hands clutching the table.

"Liz . . ." she said. "Liz, now, listen—"

I was about to explode.

"Why did you give me this?" I said, my voice low and the tail tightening around my neck. It could feel my rage. The man she was with looked confused; the sticks dropped out of his mouth and fell to the floor.

"Would you like to take a seat? We'd love for you to join us."

"I'm allergic to fish," I snapped. "Why?" I asked her. "I deserve a fucking explanation." She sighed and motioned to the door. Outside she lit a cigarette. She was so elegant, like a movie about the sixties made in the nineties.

"I'm sorry," she said. "I had no choice."

"Why would you ever give this to somebody?"

"The tail came to me five years ago, a little before I met your uncle."

"Are you guys still together? Who was that?"

"That is somebody from the past." She parted her lips and inhaled. "The tail was my best friend's. I was doing her a favor."

"Did you know what the favor was, exactly?"

"She was like my sister, and she was suffering. An ex-girlfriend's friend had given it to her. And some other woman's mother had given it to her before that. I guess the story is that long ago, a group of women were covered head to toe in hair and were given a choice: stay covered in hair or have a tail. Or maybe they all had tails, but the tails went crazy, and somebody gave them another choice: Pass the tail on, and you'll never be bothered again by hair. I don't know. Does it matter?"

"Why me?"

"My friend had just given birth, and I was visiting her, and you came in with her dinner. You were so accommodating and kind and had the hairiest arms I had ever seen. I knew it had to be you because, well, I didn't know you, and then I wouldn't feel so bad."

"So you stalked me? Do you even love my uncle? You ruined a marriage."

"Well, yes. And I think so, most days."

"I could sue you."

"Probably not. I don't think anyone would believe you. Or us. I'm sorry, Liz. You have no choice but to pass it on."

"But I don't want to make anyone else suffer like this."

"Do you want to date? Do you want to have a career? Do you want to be independent?"

"I can do that without hurting another person." She looked at me, beautiful, sad wide eyes underneath really thick eyelashes. I noticed she had no hair on her face except for where it was supposed to be. Did giving up the tail leave you smooth forever?

"Life will be very hard for you," she said.

"Life is hard for everybody!" I turned away from her. She threw her cigarette into the snow and stomped it out. She really was so elegant. A brand-new-lamp kind of woman.

"You are selfish," I told her. "You are unloving and cruel. I will never be like you." I walked away from her. She didn't respond to me, but I knew I'd gotten to her. I went to the liquor store and bought a nip of Fireball. I chugged it down and watched videos on my phone of otters getting stuck in trash in the ocean. Maybe this was just gonna be the way it was gonna be. Maybe we all had our destinies. Maybe it was written in the stars. Lucas was, of course, happy to see me.

"Wow, Liz! Cool scarf!"

"Hey, Lucas. Hey, Whoolia."

"It's Julia."

"Okay."

Lucas sat in between me and Julia. I noticed that Julia, like me, had a significant amount of facial hair. There was a certain fuzz above her lip and on her chin. *I could just give this to her now*, I thought. *I could be rid of this whole thing. Lucas could be mine, and my tail wouldn't murder him in the middle of the night.* He was really into the movie. It was French and about a woman who was about to find out whether or not she had cancer, and then it turned out she did. Lucas didn't even look at me or Julia, and both of us were trying to look at him but then just kept meeting the other's gaze and scowling. I ended up weeping over the movie, which brought the blood back into my neck, because the tail was so depressed.

"What did you think of the movie? I thought it was so fantastic!" Lucas said afterward. I was sleepy from the whiskey I had brought inside and nervous he could smell it on my breath, so I hid behind the tail.

"It was good. I'm kinda sad that she's gonna die."

"Yeah, that's so true! But at least she met somebody, right? I mean, maybe that's not important. But, wow. So depressing but also so beautiful!" Lucas looked like he was about to cry, too.

"Yeah, I really loved the mise-en-scène of the film," Julia said. Dumb bitch.

"Totally! I mean the director is really particular about framing."

"Right," I said. "Hey, Julia, can I talk to you for a second?" She seemed excited to talk to me. We went to the movie theater bathroom.

"What's up?"

"I have something that I need to give you."

"Oh, my birthday's not till next month. That's so nice, though."

"Well, I wanted to give this to you early." I plucked a hair from the tail and held it out to her.

"Is that an eyelash?"

"It's, um . . . it is a special herb that, if you keep it on you, it'll just . . ." Whoolia looked like I was telling her a joke that was too long-winded. Like I didn't know how to end it when it should be ended. I took a step closer to her so that we were almost nose to nose. I went to move my hand to her back, the plucked hair balancing on my fingertip.

"Liz," she said, laughing a little and gently tapping my shoulder, "I consider myself a bisexual woman, but I am not really attracted to women unless it's specifically a romantic situation. I am so flattered, though." I retracted my finger and my hair.

"My bad," I said, clearing my throat. "No, sorry, yeah, I hope I didn't make you uncomfortable." She smiled and opened her arms for a hug. I accepted the embrace. I couldn't be what my stepaunt wanted me to be. I had to be better than that.

The next day, I decided not to strap the tail to myself. I was losing oxygen during the day and dealing with back pains at night. I decided to just drink another shot of whiskey before work and watch *The Boy in the Striped Pajamas* on silent while listening to spoken word poetry to bum the tail out as much as I could. Work was always miserable, right? We would survive the day, the tail and me. Montgomery greeted me at the lockers, where he asked, "Are you drunk, Liz?" I grinned and told him, "No, I'm blessed." He clapped his hands together and said, "That is what I am talking about, Liz! The spirit of the Lord is through you now!" I sighed and felt the tail brush against my shin. It just looked like I had gained a little bit of weight but only in one leg. I let myself breathe deeply. Today was going to be just fine.

My last stop of the day was always the children's ward. My cart was full of sweets and chicken fingers and fries with smiley faces on them. *Yeah*, I thought, *I eat like a kid stuck in the hospital.* I made my way to room 12A, where a young boy had tubes down his throat. There was Lucas, sitting next to him in one of the hospital chairs that had a bunch of fun little shapes on them because this was the kids' ward, and kids are happy and nice and don't ever die or grow up to feel like shit. He was with an older Japanese man sitting in another fun chair.

"Dr. Liz," Lucas said to me in what he probably felt was an extraordinarily serious voice. "I was wondering if we would run into you! This is my dad—I mean, my father—and this is my little brother, Isaac. He just got his appendix removed, but he waited too long, so it ruptured during surgery. I ended up having to go to the emergency room after the movie last night. Traffic was intense." He was standing up and had his hands on his hips for some reason.

"Exciting!" I said, feeling the tail stir by my ankles. "I mean, that sucks. I'm glad he's alive." I tried to focus on the tubes down Isaac's throat and how that was sad.

"Long shift?" Lucas asked me, hands still on his hips and pursing his lips, his voice an octave lower. Why was he acting like he was selling me a car?

"Normal amount. This is my last stop."

The dad looked up at us. He opened the maroon plate of food.

"We asked for gluten-free bread. Is this gluten-free?"

"Yes, it is," I said, checking the slip.

"Great. I'm on a diet."

Lucas laughed politely and nervously.

"Dad," Lucas said. "Always concerned about your *diet*."

"I have celiac disease."

Lucas laughed like a car salesman.

"Get better soon," I said, looking at Isaac, who weakly held up two fingers.

"Well," Lucas said. "When you're all done, maybe we can take the train back together." Then he went to touch my shoulder, and that's when my pants ripped apart. The tail knocked down some get-well-soon cards and a teddy bear. The dad screamed, and Lucas did too. Isaac started choking on his tubes.

"Is that an animal?" Lucas stood with his hands above his head. I was absolutely pantsless, and the tail was slithering way above my head, ready to strike.

"Liz, is that thing . . . attached to you?"

"Yes."

"Well, can you get it off?"

"Obviously I can't get it off!" The gluten-free bread fell out of the dad's mouth. I worried I was about to get fired.

"What the hell is going on?"

"I have a tail. My aunt gave it to me in a way that wasn't consensual, but also it's hereditary, technically, in an emotional way. It's a three-foot tail that gets really excited, and it's ruining my fucking life!" I looked around me and found a hospital gown. I shook it on and left the room, leaving the cart of food there, too. I was weeping hysterically, and the tail calmed down. It was dragging now at my feet.

I got to the train station in my hospital gown. It was snowing outside. I was completely freezing and mortified. I was thinking about moving to Canada, but it's not like the tail would magically disappear as soon as I crossed the border. I would just be an illegal immigrant with a tail.

"Liz!" Lucas was running down the hill. I didn't answer him.

"Liz, let's talk!" I felt him near me. I tried to think of climate disaster, and people busking in train stations who are bad at playing their instruments, and the rising ocean tides drowning them.

"Don't come closer."

"It's okay, Liz. Listen, I used to have a huge mole on my nose, and it's all everybody ever looked at. See? You can even see the scar right there on my nose!" I turned, and he was pointing to his nose. The scar had faded to a slightly different color than his skin and was the shape of a crescent moon. Of course I had noticed the scar on his nose before. It made him hotter.

"This is kind of a different situation," I told him, moving the hospital gown over my hairless knees. The hair had completely dropped away from my body. I was smooth and hairless, like a baby or a porn star. I didn't even have my wallet. I would have to go back to the hospital eventually. What was I thinking?

"It is," he said, sighing. The tail rose out from my back and through the hospital gown. "Can I touch it?" I squirmed at the question. The "it" of it felt disgusting. "It" was a creature, and so was I.

"I don't like how you said 'it.'"

"I'm sorry."

"It's okay."

"You can say no." For the first time, he wasn't talking like a customer service worker or whatever that was inside the hospital, where I think he was just nervous. His hands were smooth and long, well-lotioned. For some reason, the option to say no made it feel okay to say yes.

"You can," I said. Lucas reached out to me like E.T. His breath spiraled out next to him in the cold. The molecules from inside his mouth danced their way to my cheeks like a kiss. He used his two fingers to poke the end, the pointiest part of the tail. It awakened, and I tried to think of death and disease, teenagers who are mean to their moms who have cancer.

"Feels kind of cool," he said. "Hey there, tail." The tail rose, and Lucas backed away. He was staring at it, tail to eye. The tail lashed at him, and Lucas winced.

"Oh no," I said, wresting the tail against my chest.

"That's okay. Let me try something different."

He opened his palm, and I wanted to dance my fingers across it, the way I did when I was a kid at my desk in school, pretending like my fingers were two professional ice-skaters doing an award-winning number across the ice to a beautiful song. Maybe it's a nontraditional ice dance to "Touch the Sky." The tail inched its way over to Lucas. It hovered. The tail stroked Lucas's face and then his ear. Lucas leaned closer. It was the closest we'd ever been to each other. He closed his eyes and breathed out. That was when the tail sliced Lucas's neck.

Luckily Montgomery was finishing up his shift and on his way to the train. He saw me carrying Lucas, who was holding his neck, and went to grab him by the legs.

"We got him, Liz!" Montgomery said. "And the Lord does, too!"

We reached the ER, where they carried Lucas away on a stretcher, blood spouting from his neck in horrible red bursts. I tied the tail around me as it went limp, because I was crying.

"Okay," I told Montgomery, "I have to go."

"I'll take care of him, Liz! I have trust in him and Him!" I went back to the train and thought about my stepaunt and how she'd been right, how I wouldn't ever be able to have a normal life. I squatted on the yellow line, releasing the tail onto the tracks. No, I wasn't planning on killing myself. In retrospect, I guess it looked like I was taking a dump. I heard the train coming and the frantic beeping from the conductor. I felt the tail tug at my back, becoming stiff with fear. I closed my eyes. I felt a pain I had never felt before in my entire life, an entire part of me I never asked for violently ripping off. Everything went black.

Don't worry. Lucas didn't die, and I didn't either, though we both will eventually. Everybody does. The train conductor stopped the train after running my tail over and carried my bloody body to the ER, where they were able to get me into surgery. The tail had been cut off horrifically, and I had lost a ton of blood. They had to give me a blood transfusion and put me in a coma. When I woke up from it, Beatrice was there, hovering over me with her pretty face.

"You almost died."

"Is the tail gone?"

"Yes," she whispered, "it's gone." Tears welled in her eyes. "I'm so sorry I did this to you."

"I'm sorry someone did this to you, too." They couldn't find the tail. When the conductor found me, I just had a massive gash on my ass. It looked like I had fallen in front of the train butt-first.

"Do you think somewhere out there," I asked Beatrice, "there's a tail?"

She started to cry. "I should have helped you more," she said. "I should've looked for another solution."

"But you said there were only two choices."

"There's always another choice. All these rules. Who cares about them?" I forgave my stepaunt Beatrice then and there. I heard someone knock on the door.

"Looks like you have a visitor." It was Lucas, with some bandaging around his neck.

"Hey, it's me."

"I know," I told Lucas. "I can see you." Beatrice swiftly left the room to give us privacy, her scarves swishing around her.

"Sorry," Lucas said, "this is just awkward."

"Why? Because you're afraid of me?"

"No." He took a seat next to me. "Okay, maybe a little bit. But maybe that's exciting!" I began to cry like a maniac. It felt involuntary, like when I visited the 9/11 Museum and picked up a phone they had set up there, and listened to a man say goodbye to his wife right before his plane crashed, and then was faced with a crumpled-up American flag at the end of the museum. The propaganda got to me, even though I was an educated person who consulted multiple news sources, and it got to me by surprise. Lucas covered my hand with his. Maybe right then, I was feeling a different kind of propaganda, the kind everyone insists isn't created by perfume companies and the blood diamond business. No, this was something to believe in.

"This was so weird," was all I could say in between sobs. "This was so fucking weird."

"It was!" he said, smiling very assuredly. Then his smile went away. He squeezed his arm. "Liz, can I ask you a question?"

"Sure," I sniffled.

"Why do you always throw out the hot chocolates I give you?"

"I'm allergic."

"To the milk?"

"No, to chocolate. And the milk. I'm allergic to everything, basically. It makes me really not fun."

"Then why do you have me make one for you every time? I mean, isn't that a little wasteful?"

"I like the routine."

"I like the routine, too." He squeezed his arm again.

"Well," he said, "maybe I can find something that wouldn't make you sick." It was the most romantic thing anyone had ever said to me.

I waited for the tail to grow back, and it didn't. I waited for it to start sprouting out of a place where I wouldn't expect it to be: my armpit, my eye. It didn't. Weeks went by. Montgomery volunteered himself for aftercare. I didn't want Lucas to see me until I was fully healed. One day I was so hungry, and Montogomery went out to grab me food. I was so delirious from the drugs, I didn't notice that it was a granola bar with chocolate in it until I was staring at the wrapper after. I began to hyperventilate.

"I'm gonna die," I told Montgomery. "I'm gonna die! Get the EpiPen!" Montgomery ran to the closet to get the EpiPen.

"Does this still work after four hours?"

"What?" I said, gasping for air.

"I gave you the granola bar four hours ago, and then you went to sleep."

"And I didn't die?"

"I don't think you're dead. Am I dead?"

"No. So if I didn't die, then what happened?"

Montgomery beamed. I knew what he was about to say.

"Liz, you are blessed!"

I asked him to make me a grilled cheese, because I wanted to see something. I told him to spice it, to make it as savory as he knew how to. I also had him bring me a jar of peanut butter and a glass of soy milk. Montgomery came back from the grocery store sweating and excited, arms full of grocery bags.

"You have the EpiPen ready, right?" I asked him.

"Yes. If I see a hive, I'll inject!"

I took a bite of the grilled cheese. The bread was nicely greased and crunchy. The cheese was sharp on my tongue. I spooned out the peanut butter and felt the fullness of it on my gums. I chewed and chewed until they were nothing in my mouth. I swallowed.

"Yup, I can feel it. I'm dying. Listen, tell Lucas—"

"Can you breathe, Liz?"

"Yeah."

"Are there bumps forming on your arms?"

"No."

"Then you are fine!"

"I'm fine?"

"You're fine."

"I'm not blessed?"

"No, Liz. You are always blessed."

Beatrice left my uncle and moved to Greece. She sent me a post-card from that island with all the statues. She wrote, *This was kind of boring. The statues are all missing limbs. I'm realizing*

history is a little boring to me! Miss you. Love, Bea (and Chandler)
(the sushi guy) XOXO

They never found the tail. Maybe the tail got to somebody else, or maybe everything ended with me. And that's kind of nice, you know? I'll never be famous, but at least I was the end, the last of them, the one who finished it all. This would be true, except for the fact that nothing ever ends, not ever. Even when we're all gone, there will be something we've left behind, something humiliating and inconsequential. The receipts of us. The old underwear.

This mustache comes today, the day Lucas and I are supposed to go to the movies. I shave it right off because I just ran out of wax. Fifteen minutes later, the mustache returns. It's a shadow on my face. Burly and consistent and obviously there. No mistaking it. And I know that no matter what I do, it'll just keep coming back. I know that this is the price I had to pay. Now, Lucas is ringing my doorbell. I rush to the door, where I see the shadow from his feet through the crack by the floor.

"Lucas, I'm just letting you know that I look a little different now. I mean, I look pretty much the same, but when you look at me, you'll notice a change."

"I don't think anything can top the tail!"

"And if you see me and don't like what you see, then that's okay. You can just tell me that."

"Liz, what's this about?"

"Just promise me you'll be honest."

"I promise!"

"Just know that I really like you and that I hope you can like me, too."

"Of course I like you! Liz, I like you so much!"

"And I'm not basing the value of myself on how beautiful you find me. Because I have already found myself. In more ways than one."

"Yeah, that's great!"

"And if you're disgusted, you can be honest. I don't want you to pity me."

"I could never pity you. Or be disgusted by you."

"Sometimes I think you're just nice to me because you're nice to everyone."

"Well, I like being nice to you the most."

"I love who I am!"

"Cool! Hey, can you open the door now? The movie starts in ten minutes."

"I'll open the door on the count of three, okay?"

"Okay!"

"And you'll be honest with me?"

"I'll be honest with you!"

Lucas is laughing. I love his laugh. I love talking to him from behind the door, and I think that I could do that forever, imagining him imagining me on the other side, and in his imagination, I am beautiful and normal and exciting and hairless all at once. And that way he can never know who I really am; he can just think me up, perfect and good, forever. But you can't live your life like that, I'm realizing. Unfortunately, you need air and unfortunately you need touch, and unfortunately you need to work and meet people there who love you, and unfortunately you need somebody to be looking at you so that you know you're still there. With your thick mustache and everything. Nothing ever ends.

"Ready?" I ask Lucas.

"I'm ready!" he says.

"One, two, three."

Dream Man

I am the man who travels through dreams. You have seen me. I could even say that you know me. They did the study; they had the people draw me—I was there. The conspiracies were right. I was hired in the 1960s by the president. Technically it's still the sixties right now, and I am traveling, getting information for something, but I cannot tell you what. They say everybody you've seen in your dreams you've seen in real life. The man sitting next to you in a dream car is a stranger you saw briefly at a deli. That is not true. I will never meet you, not ever.

You are in a video store. You are old enough to remember those, though I will not live long enough to see them in real life. You go to the children's section and stare at the *Winnie the Pooh* DVD, then the walls fall down; the DVDs turn into little birds, and one of them is big enough to carry you away. You arrive in the city, and it is raining. In the distance, you see a door in the middle of the street. I am in a coffee shop that you remember, sitting in a chair that you remember. You construct things in your dreams that you don't even know about, entire architectures, floor plans for me to walk through. I am watching through a glass window. You open the door, and it shows you your mother eating a pizza with her hair up at a roller-skating rink. Behind her there are three men in suits, and they are talking over a box. You close the door. I write something down.

Your child is drowning in a bathtub that's filled with Capri-Sun. You try to save him, but each time you reach for him, he slips away from you like a fish. The juice gets higher and higher, but there's a window on the ceiling. You crawl through it and leave him behind and feel a sense of relief, and in this dream, you can admit this to yourself. You open the window, and you are in college, listening to a psychology professor. You are late. You sit down, and your backpack is by your seat. Your future husband is next to you. He hands you a pencil. I am two rows behind you.

I sleep in a small bedroom in a building in Brooklyn that will be demolished in 1982. I know this because I have seen my landlord's future stress dreams. I pay him under the table. He never asks me how I make my money. I am pretty exhausted all the time. The dream-hopping starts to mess with you. I go on walks sometimes. I sit in a park, and I read the paper. It can be dreadful knowing everything that's going to happen. The dreams obviously reflect history. I can tell when something particularly catastrophic has happened based on how many dreams I'm in where people are naked in front of many people or running from guns or falling from somewhere very high. Of course I get the instinct to help, but there's nothing I can really do. Occasionally I am comforted knowing that there's nothing I can do, that I've been given this one job in this one life, and maybe it's a dirty job, but it brings to me to the next day, and it brought me to you.

In 1980, I see your mother. She is as gorgeous as you remember. What a beautiful twist it would've been if it turned out that I was your dad. Kind of sick, maybe. But beautiful. I follow her the whole day. She serves me a pie at a diner. She gets off work and goes to the movies. She laughs at something, then she cries. She sees me briefly in the lobby, and she recognizes me. She thinks I am somebody else. I wave back, and she realizes her mistake. I don't dream of her. I don't dream at all.

Of all the dreams, I like yours the most. You have the funniest anxieties. You are still a little in love with so many people. As a child, you have a fear of tornadoes, so you have a reoccurring dream where you are hiding in the basement from one, holding a Beanie Baby. When you're a teenager, you have a hilarious dream where the boy you like turns into a balloon animal, and when you kiss him, he pops. The day before you get into Columbia, you dream you're looking into a microscope, and inside the microscope is a purple hat. You knew you were going to get in. All that hard work. The studying.

I jump into your husband's dream, and that's how I know about the affair. It drives him crazy, if that's comforting in any way. He'll be screwing the children's kindergarten teacher, and then she'll turn into these bugs while you're set on fire nearby. The thing is, he loves her. He dreams about holding her hand on a bench. And sometimes she turns into his old girlfriend, and sometimes she turns into you. But the sky is rosy around him, and my body gets overwhelmed with his desire. The pulsing all over. It's too much for me. It makes me sick. This is when I start to meddle with things. I write, *He's cheating*, on a piece of paper. I leave it on a giant chair in the middle of a field. You see me briefly, walking away. "Who are you?" you say. I keep walking.

I've seen so many dreams. Elvis's dreams. The dreams of the fore-fathers. The dreams of the people they killed. I know what your ancestors dreamed of. I'm sorry to say it was never about you. But you do dream of them, which feels unfair. And they dreamed about jealousies, about love and death, about their daily tasks; they dreamed about what to eat the next day, and they did dream prophetically. The body can sense when doom approaches. I keep track of the prophecies: the giant birds eating their young, the bloody suns.

You are a doctor. I gather that from the dreams you have of textbooks, of cadavers neatly opening up for you, of you holding intestines in your hands, the smell of hypoallergenic soap that fills my nose. You have a reoccurring dream of a child you could not save. The child has a strange headache, and you examine him over and over again. It was a tumor, and the tumor caused an aneurysm, which happens all too quickly in your dreams, as well as the child's decay. His face peels away—he is a skull, he is grass. And there's nothing you can do.

I needed a job. I walked into an office one day, and they asked me to just observe and write things down. I was good enough at it. I was somebody who nobody would remember, they said. I wasn't ugly. I wasn't handsome. They pulled up a chart. I looked enough like anybody in any century. They gave me a TV, some radiation-resistant gloves, and a pair of glasses.

———

Yes, some people can predict the future. You are one of them, unfortunately for you and unfortunately for me. In the dream, you're holding your breasts in your hands like they're pieces of cake. They jiggle at you. When you look closer, you see a gray worm burying itself into a nipple. The worm slithers through, and the breast grows and swells, turns gray, explodes. You're surrounded by bright green mucus, and there are hospital sounds. It's very on the nose. In two months, you'll get the diagnosis.

Of course I try to stop it. I leap into the dreams of doctors and scientists of the future to see if there's anything there about a cure. There is hope, and there is failure. There are improvements for the future of humanity. There is no saving you right now.

I let myself cry about it. How stupid I am. I live in a different time. I will die the year after you are born. A woman passes me by on my bench and offers me a handkerchief.

The dreams after you leave your husband are spectacular. You're on a beach in Italy with a golden horse. All your teeth fall out on the Hollywood Boulevard. You have a brief affair with a man who is a wetlands biologist, and when you sleep beside him, he enters your dreams without knowing. He sees me in the corner of a women's dressing room, wearing a tutu, because that is how your dream places me. He comes closer and closer, and I disappear. When he wakes up, he tells you he had a weird dream about a man with a unibrow, but he doesn't say where he was, even though it was the same place you were.

You dream about the end of the world, though I can't really discern symbols from reality. There are several endings, it seems—roads that we can take or not take. A disease that takes away 1.5 percent of the population. A man drowns in his basement because of a flood. The crops turn to ash. The sun makes everybody look very, very old. To you they are just nightmares. I must write everything down.

It happens because of you. They are outside now. They've come to replace me. They will take all my notes. They will erase me from my living world. But somewhere you are still dreaming. There is a man in a long coat at the end of an auditorium. He is not here to kill you. He will not come any closer. The door is opening now. I hear the gun being cocked. Look for me. You are a child now, and the images of your day are cycling through your head, and they are building little things called memories that will help you learn language and help you be a person, the person that I love. The last dream I ever had, I was an old man, and I was with an old woman.

She did not have your face. I had seen her someplace before, as is the rule. We were on a porch, and we were laughing. I was certain in that dream that that would be my life. That I would find that woman for me and that we would be the reason the other could sleep through the night. Well, that never happened. Stuff gets in the way. Dreams die. You get a job to live a life. They are in my room now, guns pointed. I close my eyes. I wonder what I'll see.

Something Loving

Macy's mom asked us if we wanted cookies and disappeared for forty-five minutes. The whole house smelled like butter. She came out with them, all gooey and lumpy, like pieces of the world, on a plate. "I've always liked them warm," she said. Macy ate them like they weren't anything special, a chore almost, a plate of vegetables, then she returned to her homework.

When I bit into one, I had to excuse myself to go cry in the bathroom, because it was so delicious and new. I used my tongue to trace a film of brown butter forming across my teeth, then used it to wiggle the smaller tooth in the front of my mouth. Sometimes I wiggle it so much that it bleeds. It isn't a baby tooth, so I know I can't just get it back. I ate five more cookies and Macy's mom had me take the rest of them home in a Ziploc bag. I spend a lot of time at Macy's house.

Coming home, I saw my mom flipping through the notebooks again with all the blue circles and yellow dots and pink lines. "Do you want some?" I asked her, holding out the bag. She didn't even look up from those notebooks. "Oh, how nice," she said, "how nice of you to offer." She doesn't like sweet things, or spicy things, or salty things. She says they make her feel sick. She likes beige things like spaghetti and potatoes and she never bakes anything.

I went to play the video game my dad used to love to keep from feeling bad. In the game, you have to get home. You dive into a pool, then find your way to the drain. You shrink yourself to get through the drain, then the drain leads you into a pipe system. In the pipe system is a small man with a funny-looking face wearing a yellow shirt. You give him one secret so that you can keep going. You type in secrets. They don't have to be real: mine never are. *I am the lost princess of Atlantis,* I'll type. *I am half-alien.* You go through the pipes and the pipes eventually lead you into space. In space, you fight these beings, but fight them without falling through a black hole. I always fall through the hole and have to start over. I don't know what happens after the aliens. My Dad does, I think. He woke me up in the middle of the night five years ago and told me he'd finished it. "You have to keep Listening," he said. And then I don't remember what he said after that. I remember his tall figure in the dark, his mouth moving, his teeth that are bad like mine, but nothing at all of what he said. The next morning, he was gone. I haven't seen him since.

I don't know where he found this game. It lives on an unlabeled CD in an unlabeled case. He used to be a hoarder of technology and filled our house with old radios and Dell laptops, floppy disks, clunky headphones, cables. Sometimes I wanna cut up the CD and stomp on it, watch the hard shards reflect the bottom of my shoe. But I haven't and I won't.

I lost my round again. I tongued my tooth.

When I'm at school, my mom works at the supermarket. She wears gloves because she doesn't want to touch the receipts. She thinks the plastic in the receipts made my Dad go crazy. The ink.

"I heard somebody call your mom Mickey Mouse the other day," Macy said at lunch, eating a homemade sandwich.

"What, why?"

"Cuz of the gloves." I saw her mouth curl upward. She was trying to be honest with me but also joke with me. I laughed along to show her I wasn't embarrassed.

"Hey, do you wanna go to Funtastic Fridays together?"

"I can't. I have a thing with my mom."

"Oh, cool. What is it?"

"It's a family thing. We do it on the first Friday of the month. I don't know. It's stupid."

"I wanna come! Plus, I've never been to your house. You're always at mine. What's the thing you do?"

"It's called Listening."

"Yeah, that sounds dope." She smiled at me. She didn't know how much I was sweating.

I told my mom Macy was coming for Listening and asked if she could get dessert. I could see a bald spot forming in her dyed and fried hair.

"Listening is a family thing," she said, her eyes glued to the notebooks.

"I know, but can't you just make dessert?"

"I don't make dessert." I started to cry. I know she felt bad because I heard her notebook close when I walked away. I played the game with headphones on and lost again.

On Friday, my mom got everything out and set it on the table: Dad's old radio, the orange cable with the pony-tail-like fray, the blue, pink, and yellow markers; and a container of store-brand cookies that looked like Tate's cookies but were called Grate's, the name of her supermarket. She gestured to it like, *Happy?* I was, but I took them out and laid them on a plate to make them look home-made. They clanked against the porcelain. The doorbell rang, and it was Macy.

"Mom?" I said, closing the door. "This is Macy." My mom wasn't gracious the way Macy's mom was. She didn't hold out her arms and ask Macy a bunch of questions. She just said, "Hi," and gave me a look only I know. I felt deeply aware of our small house, the lack of decorations, the way it smelled like rubber gloves.

"You gotta try these cookies," I told Macy. "My mom is *such* a good baker." My mom raised one eyebrow and handed me my notebook. Thankfully she didn't say anything. She played along. I wiggled my tooth.

"Nice to meet you," Macy said, taking a cookie. "What are you *listening* for?" She didn't really care about the answer. My mother stayed silent and opened her notebook, revealing all the circular doodles and lines going all the way down. I opened mine, which had stuff like "poo poo poo" and "blah blah blah" written all over it because I don't really take Listening seriously.

"Kind of just whatever we hear," I said. My mom turned the dial to AM, and the static washed over us. She closed her eyes.

"Do you ever actually hear anything?" Macy whispered. I made sure my mom's eyes were still closed, and I shook my head. Macy crunched on the cookie. Could she tell they were from the store? I ripped off a piece of notebook paper and placed it in front of her with the markers.

"Sometimes not hearing anything at all is also part of Listening," I explained. "Basically we started doing this with my dad, and now we just keep doing it. Blue is something relatable, yellow is something to watch out for, and pink is something loving."

"Okay," Macy wrote her name in blue. "That's kind of cool. Why did your dad do this?"

"Um, my mom thinks something happened to him as a kid."

"Oh, really?" Macy asked. "Like what?" I was sweating. She wrote her name again. My mom drew the circles.

"Uh, I don't know. It also could've been how much he touched receipts?" I said.

"Receipts?" Macy asked.

"These cookies rule, Mom!" I reached for one of the store-brand cookies and bit into it with my front teeth first. There was a sick feeling of something unfastening and coming loose, gum ripping. I spit my tooth out in my hand. My mother opened her eyes.

"Oh, Vera," she said.

"Do you need help?" Macy's marker was suspended in her hand.

"Guy'll cleab ip ubp," I said. "Es bokay." I wiped my mouth with my other hand and set the tooth on the table, leaving a red handprint on the yellow cloth. I saw the orange cable twitch as if it were dancing. Its insides sparked. My mom leaped from her seat.

"Does that usually happen?" Macy asked.

"It hasn't," my mom said as she hovered her hands over the dancing cable. She seemed afraid to touch it.

"*Vera*," a voice I knew said through the radio, "*Vera, I know.*" My mom flipped through the notebook desperately, looking at the circles and the lines, even though we'd all clearly heard what the radio said, though it was unclear if it was something to watch out for, something relatable, or something loving.

"David!" she whispered to the radio, "David?" A thud on the front door. Another. "Open it!" She shook me and the tooth escaped my hand, "It could be him!"

"Is David your dad?" Macy looked from me to my mom to the radio to the door, setting her marker down, "Is this like charades?" I walked past Macy and opened the door, my bloody hand getting all over the knob, and a light flashed in my eye, as if somebody were taking a picture.

When I turned around, my mother and Macy were gone, and there was a small man with a funny face in a yellow shirt sitting at the table. He held up my bloody tooth and smiled at me. His teeth were perfect. The walls were all pink.

"Game," I managed to say, though I couldn't hear my voice. He placed a finger over his mouth and used the other to point to the radio. I heard my mom scuffling around and Macy crying, my mom shushing her, telling her to Listen.

Outside it was all blue, like my house was underwater. The man in the yellow shirt moved his finger from his mouth to the open door, letting in all that light.

"Don't you need a secret?" I asked. The blood in my mouth had dried. He shook his head, holding up my bloody tooth.

Mom? Macy? I have to go now. You know how the game goes. I don't know how long I'll be gone. I don't know if my dad really figured it out. I think there are rules, and you can get lost or stuck even if you follow them. I think things look different in real life. I think we hear what we want to. You can have the rest of the cookies. Are you listening?

But I'm Still the King

Iasked my mom if it would be possible to stay at my great-uncle's finca instead of visiting the Cristo Negro. I wanted to splay out on the hammock, rub myself with mosquito repellent, and scribble postcards to my friends about all I had experienced here in Guatemala: the way pollution stayed in your eyes, how men walked the streets with their machetes, the breathtaking mountainside in the shape of a Mayan face. "Just text them," she said impatiently. "We didn't go back in time." She reminded me again that this wasn't a vacation and that I needed to come with her and go on this religious pilgrimage as a family. I fantasized about what it would be like if I had a partner here. My family would like him, I thought. It would have to be a man because they wouldn't be able to deal with homosexuality. He would ask questions and speak Spanish, relieve me of social obligation and anxiety. A boyfriend is the ultimate buffer. Instead I was alone, with my godless tattoos and Morse code Spanish. "You need to meet my brother," she said. "And you can't leave me alone with her," she pointed with her thumb to my Abuelita, who was splashing her eye drops in. She was the whole reason we were here. Last time she visited alone, she got lost on the way back during a transfer in Houston. When she finally arrived in New Jersey at four in the morning, two flimsy blue masks over her face, eyes darting all around with anxiety, we knew she couldn't travel alone anymore.

My mom had a coughing fit then, hit her chest, then hocked a loogie onto the dirt. "Ew, Mami," I said, wrinkling my nose. She glared at me. "What? I can't help it!"

I'd been self-conscious about my mom's ugly cough on the plane, turning away from her so that people wouldn't think I approved of her spreading disease. She purchased Tusilexil at a local drugstore, a cough syrup made up of some concoction of medicines not allowed in the States, and she took generous swigs from it every few hours. It was helping but not enough. With each cough, she shook her head dramatically, rolled her eyes, and laughed. Here you laughed at everything except God. Everything was a loving jibe, and nobody was immune. When a joke was made, it never got old, and it never died. You resurrected it over and over, taking turns holding up the corpse and shaking it back to life. That's something I would've written on the postcards.

I held my Abuelita's cane as my mother and my cousin Teresa lifted her into the red van we had been driving around in. Teresa wore a slicked-back ponytail and didn't bother with makeup. She wore this green T-shirt that read *I <3 Cleveland* and had tough, thick hands and a hearty laugh that sounded like she had a perpetual beer in her grip. She had two daughters and no husband. "Better that way," she said to me with a cackle. The van was her side business, and she was heavily discounting it for us. She had secured colorful blinking lights to the front of the van, which I thought were for marketing or to invoke a party spirit but were really just to avoid crashing into another car on the dark single-lane roads at night. All the big cars had party lights and made the highway look like Christmas. When a sparkling sixteen-wheeler would advance toward us, Teresa and I would lock eyes in the mirror, and she'd give me a wink. The wink made me feel safe; we were in her hands.

We rolled down the dirt road, the car swaying hypnotically. I took a shaky video of cows scattered around the glossy mountainside. "He's meeting us at the bottom," my mother told Teresa, who gave her the colloquial "ah-ha."

Teresa nearly ran Tio Ramos over. "Puchica," she said, slamming the brakes. He was standing in the middle of the road, one bony hand sticking out in a greeting. A button-down hung loose around his chest, tucked into faded jeans held up by a silver belt buckle. My mom flung the door open and sprinted out. He held on to her sun hat, and they swayed back and forth, the window of the van framing them cinematically. I took out my phone to record the moment. They hadn't seen each other in thirty years. It had been enough time for two generations of family pets to be adopted and then die; for descendants of finished wars to start them again; for child stars to grow up and hypersexualize themselves to prove they were adults; for those same child stars to check into rehab and then reemerge with an anthem single moms who grew up listening to them could scream to in their cars in Target parking lots, wondering how life came to be this way. A tear dripped down my cheek as I thought about the force of time and how sad Target parking lots were. A sulfuric smell filled the car then, putrid and skunk-like. My Abuelita was trying to yank the door open to join them. I realized she had farted.

"Are you coming?" I asked my cousin, sniffling. She looked up from her phone and shook her head. "Nah," she said.

The thing was, Tio Ramos had been excommunicated from the rest of the family, and no one would really tell me why. He had done something unforgivable and was no longer allowed on my great-uncle's property. My mind cataloged all the awful things he could've done: Stolen from the family. Murdered somebody. Molested a child. Whatever it was, my mom didn't want to talk about it. It was better, she said, if I didn't know. My Abuelita spent a lot of time crying over him and his situation, which, from what I could understand, was just being a loser. She held her veiny hands together when she saw him, shaking her head and sobbing.

I got out of the car, and my uncle hugged me with the same fierceness with which he'd hugged my mother. He smelled like cinnamon and sweat, the way all the men here did. He held me by the shoulders and looked me up and down. "You stole your mother's face," he said, cupping his hand over my cheek. I was thinking the same about him. I was stunned by how much he looked like my mother. Despite his deeper copper-colored skin, he had the same lashed eyes and bone structure, the same sloping mouth and prominent nose. He was handsome in the way that my mother was beautiful. If it weren't for his missing front teeth, he would look like a movie star, a man trotting in on a horse to save the day, a pistol at his side. I tried my best not to look at the dark gap in his mouth, the rot that began where the remaining teeth were.

After we all wiped away our tears, we climbed back into the van, and he sat next to my Abuelita, wrapping his skinny arm around her. "How wonderful it is," he said, "to see la monjita again." My mother turned in her seat and smiled sheepishly. It was so weird to see her act like a little sister. The family called her la monja instead of Fernanda, because she'd arrived in this world white like the national flower. It was also because it pissed her off, which was why most nicknames stuck. My mom started coughing again, whacking her chest with her open palm. "You okay?" my uncle asked. My mom shook her head. "I'm fine," she said hoarsely. "It just won't go away."

I didn't know if I should keep my distance from Tio Ramos or not. I could sense that he felt my apprehension when he asked me about my life. Teresa was stone-faced and silent, her big smile zapped away with my uncle in the car. The silence seeped into all of us as we stared wordlessly out the windows. I felt guilty for making her be in the same car as him just so we could go see the Cristo Negro. "So . . . why is the Jesus Black?" I asked the car, trying to make conversation, but my Spanish made it sound like the opening of some fucked-up joke. "Because He's Black," my Abuelita answered matter-of-factly. We had all thought she was asleep. Teresa burst out laughing, and my mother and uncle did, too. "Don't be so racist," Teresa told me, her eyes narrowing and then bouncing back as she let out one of her cackles. We all laughed together. I had broken the silence at my expense. The real reason, I found out using the hot spot in Teresa's van, was the oxidation from ash smoke. But it also could've been the Spanish colonizers trying to convert a pagan god into the one true King of Kings. Of course. It was a fucking ruse. A lie. I didn't want to tell anyone that. Out the window, a truck with a group of men lying on the roof with their arms behind their heads drove by. A baby slept peacefully in his mother's arms on the back of a motorcycle. The mother locked eyes with me and kept them there, unafraid to show me that I was a stranger.

I squirmed in my seat, my thighs sticking together. My period had just started, and it felt like my guts were falling out while someone was yanking my fallopian tubes like they were a rope. I had purchased a dainty Tampax box at JFK, thinking I would only use half of it, but I was already on my last one. Any doubts I had about having a gringa stomach were confirmed when my family kept lovingly thrusting food upon me every two hours. The heaps of sugar and cream. The tortillas and chicharrones sprinkled with chiltepe. The gigantic bowls of caldo and the collagen slipping off the bone. All of it went straight into the toilet. I felt that the diarrhea was proof I didn't belong here. Every runny stool was evidence that I would go away soon. Every seat on the toilet was a small peck goodbye.

As soon as we reached the viewpoint at Esquipulas, I booked it to the bathroom. I paid the attendant five quetzales, she handed me a bundle of toilet paper, and I ducked into a stall and relieved myself. I tugged the tampon out of me, and saw how exhausted it was from my blood. I had a brief fantasy about having a miscarriage. It was a fantasy because I hadn't slept with anyone in months, and I was approaching an age of rusty eggs and collagen creams. What was I going to do, text the last person I'd slept with that it hadn't worked this time, sweetie, that we should try again, my lovebug, that it could fix everything, baby? I was getting older, but what kept me young, I felt, was my loneliness. There was possibility inside it. There was someone, somewhere, brewing who wouldn't disappoint me. I tossed the tampon into the trash can with my soiled toilet paper. I stuck in another tampon and prayed it had enough strength to last me until the end of the night.

"People used to crawl here on their knees," my mom said, pointing at the severe, beady stones making up the ground of the white basilica, "bleeding. We would watch them." She squinted her eyes, pursed her lips. "Try it," she told me abruptly. "Get on your knees. See how it feels." She looked at me all serious, but then her face broke into a laugh, which turned into a cough, another shaking of the head, an eye roll. "You try it, pendeja," I said. She glared at me. "What did you say?" my Abuelita asked, her hand clutching my uncle's arm. I pictured us all stumbling up the stairs, the skin on our knees flapping open with blood.

We entered a mass that had already started. I think that except for my Abuelita, we had all forgotten it was Sunday. Heads turned as my mom coughed while she tried to find an open seat. "Excuse me," she said, coughing. "So sorry." My uncle motioned for us to follow him to the back, where a man holding an AR-15 let us into a snaking path that would lead us to the Cristo Negro. We shuffled in slowly because of Abuelita and her cane, passing by different depictions of miracles of the Cristo Negro and Jesus Himself. There was one of His face made up of different coins that people had tossed into the offering space. In another He was a mannequin behind glass on all fours, His hair (real human hair, my mother told me) sticky with blood hanging like a curtain in front of His face. I let out a snort. "Bless you," my Abuelita said. I mean, it was hilarious to me: Jesus was that girl from *The Ring* crawling out of a TV; He was Lady Gaga screaming "Paparazzi" at the VMAs; He was horror; He was camp. A little depression fell over me because I had no one to share this with. I shook my head. I was a child of the internet and not a child of God. And anyway, I wasn't a child anymore.

We made it finally to the Cristo Negro. He lived inside a plexi-glass box behind the altar, His emaciated body propped up on a golden cross, golden rays shining from His head, which hung with exhaustion and love, as a martyr's does. Three marble figures were beneath Him, white and praying, one hanging on to His cross like a girl in love. Looking at the light shining on Him and hearing the braying organs, I felt a rush of something that I wasn't expecting. I was in awe, and I was very small, and I thought about how I'd felt that one time I'd taken a hike up a mountain upstate, how I had been breathless taking in all that I had climbed for, the unflinching beauty that didn't give a shit about me. I'd also felt that way, I thought, at an emo reunion tour.

The mass was still happening, the priest listing off people to pray for. We stood behind the altar with our backs to everybody. My mother went first, kneeling and closing her eyes. When she stood up, she let out a few gravely coughs into her fist. Then my Abuelita went, clasping her hands together and whispering and shaking her head. Her eyes began to water, and my uncle went to hug her. My mom let out a frustrated sigh. She hated her dramatics and felt she didn't really have anything to cry for, given all the doctors' appointments she took her to and vitamins she made her take. She had clawed her way up the immigration dream, and all my uncle had to do was be Abuelita's one precious son. I felt myself pulled to say a prayer in Spanish. Tears came to me again as I thought about how all we had in this small life was believing in something.

Then my uncle went. I watched him stand in front of the Cristo Negro and then swivel around in his cowboy boots to look at the mass. I watched his mouth curl. He was humored by them, I felt, the pathetic bunch here to pray for a job, for their son's safe passage into the States, for a lump to go away, for the salvation of their young daughter's soul. He turned back and stared at the Cristo Negro, his eyes wide open.

We had to walk backward on our way out so that our backs wouldn't be to Jesus. My mom held on to a coin and closed her eyes, muttering something, then tossed it toward the offering section, where various coins and bills littered the ground. I felt my cynicism return. This was just another way to make money. I watched a Mayan family with flashing red lights strapped onto their cowboy hats recite prayers from a worn booklet as they stepped backward. Their children didn't care, running around them like bees.

We were getting hungry, so my mom suggested Pollo Campero. We walked through the cobblestoned streets, passing eloteros and Venezuelan migrants selling Bon Bon Boms. *I'm halfway there*, the signs read. *Help me on the rest of my journey.* I paid for a mystery flavor and unwrapped it. There was a yellow critter sleeping there, curled around the sweet globe. I chucked it to the ground.

"I think a few of these opened up in New York," I told my mom. She looked annoyed. "This is the real thing," she said. "You won't find anything like it. You can't even come close." When she asked for a pitcher of Gallo, the waitress, a bored-looking woman with blond spaghetti streaks in her black hair, flatly said they didn't serve them anymore after the pandemic. "Well, give us the order that everybody loves," my mom said cheerfully. "The most popular one!" The waitress said, "Crispy," with a shrug. When the piles of crispy chicken arrived, my mom took an enthusiastic bite, closing her eyes and relishing in the taste. "Mmmmm," she said as she ate, but her eyes started darting around. Then her face slowly fell. She moved the chicken from one side of her mouth to the other. She swallowed. "This wasn't the right flavor," she said, but I'm not sure to who. "That waitress doesn't even want to be here." I didn't really have an opinion on the chicken, only that it was sitting poorly in my stomach.

Tio Ramos asked my mom if we'd like to join him for dinner tomorrow night with his family. She took an unnecessary sip from her Coca-Cola and made up an excuse about how we needed to be at the airport. I felt it: The magic of the reunion was already gone. "But I promise I'll see you before we head back. I have something for you." He blinked at her.

Teresa sat next to me, ravaging her chicken and not looking any of us in the eye. She didn't want to be there and was pretending my uncle wasn't. She left her plate clean and extracted a few quetzales for my mom, who shoved it back into her calloused hand and told her not to insult her. My cousin sighed, wrapping the bills up and stuffing them back into her purse. She told us she'd wait for us in the van. "Bye-bye," my uncle said in English. "Seeyoulayer." My cousin acted as if a mosquito had just woken her up, humming with her blood. She showed him her teeth then excused herself.

Ordering another Coca-Cola, my mom was hit with another coughing attack. It was sounding worse and worse, like there were wet pebbles jumping inside her throat. She waved her hands in front of her face and rushed to the bathroom. I was left with my sleeping Abuelita and my uncle, who I felt staring at me. He hadn't touched his food. I took another bite of chicken so I wouldn't have to say anything. Behind him on the wall, the Pollo Campero chicken had his yellow feathered arms open, as if welcoming me into a loving embrace.

"Do you want to see something?" I heard my uncle say. I looked up. His eyes were so dark and large. My Abuelita was snoring beneath her big sun hat. Next to us, a group of rich Guatemalans with vacant eyes and pristine white shoes rested their heads in their hands, twirling the straws in their Coca-Colas.

"Sure," I said. He snatched the last chicken wing and shoved it in his mouth for two seconds, then, with two fingers, plucked out a shiny, clean bone. I didn't see him swallow. I tried my best once again not to look at the hole in his mouth. I laughed politely. "That was funny. How did you do that?" I asked, then he said something I didn't understand, a jumble of Guatemalan phrases clapped together. "Really?" I managed to say, the bone laid out on a napkin, all shiny, like it was on display after an archaeological dig. "Very cool." I pulled out my phone to connect to the Pollo Campero Wi-Fi. My stomach was twisting around. I decided I didn't like my uncle and didn't want to be around him, and I didn't care if he picked up on that.

When my mom came back from the bathroom, I asked if everything was okay. "Let's go," she said, flinging her bag over her shoulder. I told her she needed to speak to her doctor as soon as we got back. "What's the matter?" my uncle said. "I can help you if you want." But my mom didn't want any of his help. She lived in the United States, she said, and that was where she would get real, legitimate help. From a *doctor.* "All right, then," my uncle said.

Before heading back, my mom wanted to show me where they used to sell candies at the market. "Why do you need to show her that?" my Abuelita said, her cane propelling her through the cobblestones. "Let that go." My mom had been miserable as a child; she's always told me that. She was more of a way for Abuelita to outsource her labor than a daughter. My mom's childhood memories weren't anything like mine, years of gleefully sitting in front of cakes with my frosted name and falling asleep in the back of a car after a day at a theme park.

The sun had already set, and the market was quieting down. Indigenous attendants listed the names of the goods they were selling in monotone chants, holding out beaded purses and key chains with quetzales on them. I liked the little items: the jewelry boxes made of wood with La Virgen carved on the front, hats with random photos of eagles sewn on, T-shirts that said *YOTUBE PELO.* "This is what we sold," my mother told me, holding up a white block of candy with the Cristo Negro engraved into it. It was encased in plastic wrap and secured with a tie at the end like a sausage. "Do you remember, Ramos?" My uncle had his hands behind his back, shuffling down the aisle in his cowboy boots. He didn't hear her. My Abuelita held on to her cane and stared into space. "Do you want one?" I asked, pulling out a quetzal. "No," my mother said, and after examining it eye to eye, she smiled and placed it back into its spot in the pyramid of sugar. Something about this annoyed me because it felt like she was pretending to be in a movie, like there was a camera focused on the far-off look in her eye. Maybe my Abuelita was right. Maybe she should just let this go.

I wandered away, looking for something to take home. I picked up a wooden key chain that had a church burned into it. It was fun, in a gothic way. "You think that's gonna help?" I turned and saw my uncle behind me. "Maybe," I said. He bowed his head so I could see his horned hairline.

"What did you ask for?" he said. I told him, "Good health for my family." I was vague. "But what do *you* want?" he asked me, one cowboy boot clopping in front of the other. I smelled him again. I squeezed the key chain. "A good career, I guess." I swallowed. "Love." We were alone in the aisle. The key chains jingled. The purses seemed to rattle with breath. He was growing taller in front of me, towering over me with that hairline. "Is that it?" he said, his eyes large and black. He, my mother, and I—we all had the same face. "Are you sure?" Leather belts swayed, and I thought I saw a gecko roaming among the merchandise. I gulped, my heart thumping in my chest. "One or the other," he said, winking at me. I chose silently in my head.

Just then, I heard my mom screaming for me. "*Graciela!*" she shrieked. "*Where the hell are you?*" She found me and my uncle, who stuck up his bony hand and grinned, the gap in his teeth showing again. He was back to his normal size, or maybe he'd just stepped away from me. "We're just over here talking," he said.

"This isn't New York. You can't wander off alone here," she said, not noticing my grandmother puttering off a few steps behind her. "She's just a girl." My uncle looked at me, a woman in her thirties, and raised an eyebrow.

"She wasn't alone," he said.

"Let's go," she said, throwing a biting look his way. "I don't want to be here anymore." Teresa was waiting for us in the van. She helped my Abuelita in again and then asked me how it was. "Good," I said. She searched my eyes, then looked away. "Ah-ha," she said.

My uncle offered me his hand and lifted me into the van, winking at me again. I didn't know what was going on, truthfully. Was my uncle a magician or something? He didn't seem important enough to be the Devil. *It's just weird here*, I thought. *It's just a weird day, and I'm on my period.* I was rocked to sleep in the van, my period cramps finally subsiding, and the day's trip taking a toll. Teresa played Vicente Fernandez and my Abuelita crooned along. In between the hour of being asleep and awake, I heard my mom violently coughing again. "Caramba, Tia," Teresa said. "Take more Tusilexil." My mom gave her a thumbs-up, twisted open the bottle, and chugged. I fell asleep again, then woke up to my Abuelita snoring, her mouth slacked open. My uncle was gripping my mom's shoulder and whispering something, his words tiny fairies crawling out of his mouth. I rubbed my eyes. My mom shook her head. He whispered again, the fairies cartwheeling, dancing.

"No, Ramo," my mother said. We went over a bump, and the car bounced, my head hitting the ceiling. My Abuelita remained asleep. But in front of me, in the seats ahead, were two teenagers. My mom's skin was rounder, and her hair was bouncier, no longer dry from dyeing it for decades. It was luscious. Alive. My uncle had all his teeth and more meat on his bones. He was handsome—my mother with a mustache. She sucked in air, and he took this hesitation as an opportunity. He closed his eyes and kept whispering, his hand on her throat. Did they know I could see? Was I even seeing anything? I tried to stay very still. He removed his hand, and she took a deep breath. They were adults again. Middle-aged, cells slowing their brakes. He grinned and patted her on the back.

"Mi monjita," he said. "She'll be fine soon." She turned from him and looked out the window. I couldn't see anything—the night had engulfed the mountains. My eyes closed again.

Tio Ramos signaled for us to stop at a point in the road that had no lights. "Here is good," he said. He pecked my Abuelita goodbye and waved at me and my mom with his rickety hand. "A pleasure to meet you," I said in my grade-school Spanish. He laughed at that. "You, too," he said. "I'll see you tomorrow," my mom called out. "On our way out. I promise." We watched him disappear into the trees.

We made our way up the mountainside, the van at a nearly 90-degree angle. I was trying to connect to the hot spot in my cousin's van when my mom was hit with another coughing attack. This time, she sounded like she was vomiting. "Mami?" I said, clapping her on the back like she was a newborn baby. "You okay?" She shook her head, gasping for air. She kept coughing. "Mami?" She wasn't responding to me. I saw her tongue wagging wildly out of her mouth and her face turning purple. She hit the window with her palm. "Stop the car!" I yelled to my cousin. "Something's happening!"

Teresa pulled the van over with a screech. I wrenched open the sliding door and led my mom out by the arm. She banged on her chest, her eyes bloody and watering. Was her throat closing? Teresa leaped behind my mom and began performing the Heimlich maneuver, her palms thrusting into her stomach, but my mom shoved her away. "Hija?" my Abuelita said, gripping her cane. "What's going on with you?" I felt my hands go numb and wondered if I was about to watch my mother die, if I was going to have to care for my grandmother, if I was going to end up all alone. My mother fell to the ground on all fours, the balls of her hands digging into the dirt. She was spitting and retching, clawing at her throat. I was completely frozen.

"Tia?" Teresa said, on her haunches. "Look at me, Tia." She gestured for me to get down on the ground with her. My Abuelita called for us to grab her, too, but we didn't have time. "I'm always getting left out of things," she mumbled. Teresa instructed me to grab her bottle of water from the car and pour it over my mother's head. I did as I was told and watched the water soak my mother's hair. My mother kept gasping for air, the water making her hair stick to her forehead in chunky strands. She was crying now. Her eyes were wild, looking at me desperately, pleading with me to do something. "What's happening, Mami? I don't know how to help you if I don't know what's happening." I was so useless. I felt something warm swimming down my leg. I reached down, and when my hand returned, it was thick with my mucky blood, clotty brown snail flesh.

My mother heaved, her back arching, moving as gelatinously as a cat's. "You got this," my cousin instructed. "Con ganas!" As if she knew exactly what the fuck was going on. "What's happening?" I said, looking at Teresa, who was coaching my mom with her hands, motioning for something to come out. My mother nodded as white foam bubbled out of her mouth. I saw something crawl from her throat to her mouth, stretching against the skin and making her face expand horrifically. Her mouth dilated into a wide square shape, like it was holding a harmonica. "Come on," my cousin said. "Come on." My mother's eyes shut, and I heard her screaming beneath all the air fighting its way in and whatever was fighting its way out. "Aruunggrhhk," she moaned. It was like she was being kidnapped by something inside her body, like an invisible man had his hand inside her and was choking her from the inside while she was yelping for help. "One more," my cousin said. "You can do this!" My mom shook her head and pounded her fist on the ground as her cheeks filled with whatever was moving up her throat. With one big shriek, my mother pushed a slimy rectangular white thing out of her mouth and spit it out onto the dirt. She collapsed next to it. The thing was sizzling with her stomach acid. I wondered if it was a tonsil stone or something. It had little bits of fried chicken clinging to its edges, blood webbing across it, and a plastic knot tied at the end like a sausage. Slowly my mom's raggedy breaths began returning to normal.

I peered at it. It had an engraving of the Cristo Negro. "What the fuck?" My mom rubbed her chest. "What is that, Graciela?" she croaked. "Let me see." I looked closer. It was the candy bar from Esquipulas. My mother darted her eyes to me, then to Teresa and my Abuelita, the scarlet color finally leaving her face. My blood was streaming down my leg at this point, pooling in my Uniqlo sock.

"Puta," my Abuelita said suddenly from the car.

I let out a snort. Teresa clapped and howled. "For the love of *God*!" she yelled. My mom was wheezing again, but this time with laughter. I held on to my stomach with my bloody hand, choking back tears. I was laughing so hard.

We understood that the only thing we could do was bury it. Teresa dug the hole, and my mother dropped the candy bar in. Abuelita patted the dirt down with her cane. We all held hands and hung our heads. Abuelita recited the Hail Mary.

"So what happened?" Teresa asked my mom as we rolled up the road again. "You forget to chew?" We laughed and laughed again, clucking like chickens. I wasn't sure if we would tell the family about what happened when we returned. I had a feeling that it would be something else unspoken. And anyway, there was never any opportunity. When we arrived at the finca, our family was waiting with goodbye mariachis and balloons. Teresa found a pad for me to use and insisted I give her my shorts for her wash in the morning. We drank more Gallos and ate more tortillas and danced with one another, bouncing and kicking up our heels. "How was Esquipulas?" my great-aunt asked. "Beautiful," I said. "Very moving."

The next morning, stuffing our dirty laundry and sneakers caked with mud from the finca into plastic bags, my mom asked Teresa if we could go directly to Tio Ramos's house on our way back to the airport, because he wasn't answering the phone. She had a suitcase of things for him that she'd brought from the US:

flashlights and a blow-up mattress, other bullshit she believed he needed.

"I need to see him before we go," she said, seeing Teresa's shoulders tense up. "I know you don't want to see him, but—"

"Tranquila, Tia," Teresa said, jangling her keys. "No tengas pena. He's your brother."

We said a tearful goodbye to my great-uncle and the rest of my family, promising to call when we arrived in the States. I pulled on the shorts Teresa had washed for me. They were stiff from air-drying, but all the blood had been washed out. The van lurched down the mountain again, taking a turn down the road we'd picked Tio Ramos up from the day before. We arrived at a brick wall with a tall metallic gate that had rust on its edges.

"We're here," Teresa said. We hobbled out of the van. I checked my ass for sweat marks. Two pregnant dogs with fleas bouncing off their bodies and pus leaking from their nipples ran up to me. I let them sniff my hand, and then, seeing their bloodshot eyes, I took it back. My mom took out her phone and dialed her brother. "He's not picking up," she muttered, pacing back and forth. I wondered if my uncle had any neighbors. The van chortled gray fumes into the air. There was nobody around. "Try again," my Abuelita said. My mom stood on her tiptoes and tried to peer over the gate. She dialed him again. My Abuelita was perched next to her with her cane propping her up, shaking it occasionally at the dogs wandering around. My mom placed her hands on her hips, the white pants she had been wearing the entire trip still free of any stains.

"Help me get the suitcase out of the van," she said finally, her face unreadable. My mom took a deep breath, inhaling and exhaling with ease.

"What if somebody steals it?" I asked.

My mom snapped, "Then somebody fucking steals it, and it's not my problem anymore. Let's go." Teresa helped us lug the suitcase beside the gate, and my mom redid her hair, stray grays coming loose. She said something under her breath. "We should wait," my Abuelita said. "I want to say goodbye to my son." My mother pinched the space between her eyebrows. "Mamá, for the love of God. He's not coming." My Abuelita started to cry again, as she had in the church and often did when she didn't get her way. I squeezed her small shoulders, and she clutched my hand with her arthritic fingers, each painted an electric blue. "She doesn't understand," she whispered. "Your mother doesn't understand." More dogs surrounded us, their tails ticking. "Come on," my mother said. "Let's go." We helped Abuelita back into the van. My mother turned around as we left the aldea, her hands clutching the gray seat. She looked like somebody's little sister again, her lashes like a cow's, her eyes big and wet and disappointed. She was a little sister, I guess. She still is.

She turned back, facing Teresa. I felt like I had to keep watch for her, so I looked behind me. I searched for a tall brown man with a pistol at his side, dust circling around him and the dogs. I waited to see him throw the suitcase over his shoulder and walk away from us, grow smaller and smaller as we drove away. But

I saw nothing. Just the road and its dirty dogs. I heard my mom sniffle and saw her wipe something away from her eye. I placed a hand on her shoulder. It was all I could do. My Abuelita looked the other way.

We ate Pollo Campero again before the airport, this time ordering the original flavor and somehow, several bottles of Gallos. Teresa shook me back and forth when we said goodbye. "May God protect you," she said to me, looking into my eyes like she was searching for something. It had been said to me so much this trip that it felt casual, an everyday wish over the phone. She waved at us until we reached security, crying.

On the airplane, we buckled my Abuelita into her seat, and she took off her sandals, her dry, warped feet wiggling next to her jacket. As we lifted off, we all held hands. My stomach gargled and cramped up from the altitude. It was a red-eye, and we only had four hours to try to sleep. "Mami?" I asked her as she was trying to manipulate her coat into a pillow. "Yeah?" she said. "Are we ever gonna talk about the candy? And Tio Ramos?" My mom pushed the coat into a flimsy ball. "What's there to talk about? It's just your uncle's babosadas. Same shit all the time. Why do you think I didn't come here for thirty years?" she muttered to herself, trying to fall asleep. Her cough had stopped completely. They lowered the lights, and the flight attendant walked through the aisle, her gloved hand sliding across the baggage compartments to make sure they were sealed. I heard Abuelita snoring. Everyone on the plane found sleep but me. I watched a stupid rom-com I had seen before, the familiar emotional beats soothing some minor anxiety I had during turbulence.

At our gate Abuelita needed to pee. "I already peed a little bit," she said, "on the plane." My mom groaned. My stomach was still cramping. As I was refilling my water bottle, I heard a clopping sound, and my heart raced again. I backed away and felt a little warm body bump into me, making me lose balance. I fell, my metallic water bottle smacking the ground, the sound echoing like a gunshot through the terminal. A hand appeared in front of me, bronzed and knuckly. I accepted it, and he lifted me up. "You okay?" he said, his voice like gravel and velvet. In his eyes I saw a bottomless lake surrounded by mountains, flecks of white that could've been boats leading its people from one dock to the other. He had silky brown hair down to his shoulders. I rubbed the arm I'd broken my fall on and stared at him, recognizing something in him. When you know, you know, I guess. It was him. It was who I had been waiting for, the person brewing for me. I heard clopping to my left and saw a small child with cowboy boots running to his mother. "I'm Graciela," I said. He told me his name, and that was when I shit myself. The shart blew out of my ass in one triumphant honk, the poorly digested preplane Pollo Campero splashing onto my sneakers, the noise of my return raising itself into the sky.

Community Hole

After my father fell from eight stories at a construction site, his helmet slipping and his skull smashing in on the cement, I sang "Fix You" by Coldplay on a children's keyboard at the funeral. My family told me I should go on *American Idol*, their eyes red with grief, their breath hot with aguardiente. This was always the moment they pointed to when they found out I got a little famous, heard one of my songs with Karma Queens in a commercial. *So proud of you, amor!* the WhatsApp message read. *We know your Papi would be, too!* I don't know if he would be proud of my career going to shit or this manic haircut I gave myself for control. He would probably be happy I was on my way back to Boston but confused about why. So much would be confusing to him, actually. You have to explain so much to dead people. I don't believe in ghosts. Believing they're real is believing the world is full of magic, and the world's full of dog piss. God, I hope I don't run into anybody. If they say they recognize me, I'll say, *No you don't*. If they ask me about Jo or the fan, I'll say, *Who are those people?*

At South Station I roll my suitcase through the freshly mopped platform (somebody just puked) and shoot my friend Arnold a text with the flip phone I bought after the forty-sixth DM telling me to kill myself. *I'm here!* I put an exclamation at the end of the sentence so that I don't seem ungrateful to sweet, dependable Arnold. I haven't slept in two days. I pass the Au Bon Pain, the Starbucks, the drug addicts and their lumpy bags, the commuters and their suitcases, craning their necks at the giant screen, waiting to be called to their destinations. I uncap my Dasani water bottle and sip the spit and particles of plastic left at the bottom.

Arnold is outside the station in his white Fiat, a pale arm branching out the window. Sweet, dependable Arnold. He waves. He looks skinnier since the last time I saw him. Pointy.

"Nice haircut. I hadn't seen it."

"I deleted Instagram." I can smell my armpits' sweat curdling from the long bus ride and the unexpected September heat.

"Noticed that. How is everything with, like, everything?"

"I don't wanna talk about it, if that's okay."

"Missed you, dude."

I've been a bad friend, or an absent one. "I missed you, too. And now we're roommates!"

"Oh yeah, about that." Arnold takes the luggage from me. He presses a button on his keys, and the car beeps, the jaws of the trunk flying up.

"What?"

"I'm moving in with Caroline, dude!" He shuts the trunk with finality. I forgot about the late-night text Arnold sent me six months ago, the screenshot of that girl from an app whose face I can't even conjure in my head. Stupid, lovesick Arnold. My only ally in Boston has abandoned me for a plushy pair of tits.

"That's so great." I'm going to cry.

"Dang, don't sound so happy for me." Arnold adjusts his rear-view mirror. His eyes stay there, like someone's in the back seat with us. I shift in my seat, my ass sweaty and sore.

"I'm genuinely happy for you." A cyclist without a helmet grows bigger in the side-view mirror. I think of suddenly opening the door and watching him fly. "When do you move?"

"Today."

"What the fuck?"

"It's just something I have to do."

I unclench my jaw.

"You wanna listen to something?" He holds out the aux cord and his phone to me, an offering. "You can listen to whatever you want." I tell him I don't have a smartphone anymore for safety reasons. Arnold puts in a Radiator Hospital tape he has, and we listen together, pretending like it's still 2015 and we're working in Harvard Square, folding shirts and serving burnt coffee, an entire day hanging on a basement gig, and nothing ever changed, and nothing ever will, and we understand the lyrics but haven't lived them yet.

THE PAINTING IN THE BATHROOM

The house is called Gray Haus, and it's gray, as the name suggests. Three stories tall, with a lawn in the front and grass that rises to our knees, dandelions glancing at us out of the green. A large, unkempt porch looms in front of me with floorboards like crowded teeth. Abandoned objects rest here: a blond mannequin with a missing eye, old sneakers in a birdcage, rusted folding picnic chairs, ceramic bowls turned into ashtrays. I get a sneeze attack.

"Bless you," Arnold says. "You need help with that suitcase?" I tell him no, but he takes it from me—sweet, dependable Arnold.

The air's damp in here, like I'm inside somebody's cigarette-infused mouth. To my right is a room full of multicolored pillows. That's it. Just pillows. To my left is a room that's empty except for a wooden piano. A staircase winds before me with a white banister. Frayed yellow papers line the wall. Old notes, doodles. A shapeless metal sculpture hangs from the ceiling.

"How's it so cold in here?" I say, touching my fingertips to my cheeks. I make my way up the stairs.

"Yeah, heat doesn't work. You have to be good about wearing sweaters." That doesn't explain why it's freezing. I reach a hall lined with more papers and photos that remind me of flaking skin. I want to lotion the walls with a fresh coat of paint. I try not to think of the comfortable loft I lived in with Jo, the renovated tile floors and the giant bay window facing the Hudson River.

"Which one is mine again?" I yell, hearing my voice echo.

"Last one on the right!" The hall's walls stretch out before me, two flaky white arms. On the floor there's a hole, large enough for a mouse to slip through. I stop by the corners of it and kneel.

"That's the hole," a voice says. A lanky guy with an eyebrow piercing stands in a doorway. The smell of patchouli wafts through the crack between his arm and the room behind him, which has a red glow to it, like it's completely lit up by candles even though it's the middle of the day. "It's always been there. We don't know when it first appeared. I got my whole foot stuck in it once." He lifts up his foot, nestled in a fuzzy white house slipper. "Sometimes it grows bigger, and sometimes it shrinks. It's a temperature thing. But now I barely notice it. You learn to walk knowing that the hole is there, but you don't make it part of your whole life. Ha. Whole life."

"Farah," I say. I stick out my hand. His nose is slightly hooked and looks a little askew. "Is it safe?" I ask, in a house that probably has hundreds of fire code violations.

"For sure. Nobody would live here if it weren't safe. I'm Bell," he says. He reaches for me enthusiastically, the way a star athlete would, but when I go to grab it, his hand's all limp, like I'm shaking a fin. I don't like it. It feels like his hand isn't just asleep but dead. He nods his head awkwardly and dips back into his glowing room. I walk through the hallway, the floors creaking beneath my boots. I rub my hands on my sweatpants, hoping to warm them up. I sneeze again.

I arrive at the last door on the right at the end of the hallway, wiping my hand on my sleeve and pulling on the moist doorknob. Light floods the room. A white candle melts into one of the windowsills, as lumpy as a tumor. A mirror that might've once hung above a fancy dining hall now rests against another flaky wall. Arnold's old mattress is on the floor, and his seafoam-colored dresser sits next to it. I'm trying to think about how nice the light is in here—because otherwise I'm gonna be too focused on how sad the mirror is against the wall and how sad all this is—when I hear little thuds from the ceiling. It's like someone's dancing. Or two people, dancing back and forth with each other. A tango, maybe. A waltz.

"Here you go," Arnold says, his face dripping with sweat from dragging my suitcase up the stairs. He balances his hands on his knees and wheezes. Upstairs, the dancing stops.

"How many people live here again?" I unzip my bag and prop it easily on the mattress.

"A lot of them come and go. I told them all about you, though." Arnold stares behind me. I follow his gaze and see only the tumor candle on the windowsill. "Yeah, they're really excited to get to know you."

"How much did you tell them?" I don't want to face questions or accusations or conjure up what our label told us to say before they dropped us.

"Oh, just that you're chill." He takes out his keys, and his hands shake, fumbling with a silver skeleton key. "I can never take these off," he mumbles to himself. "And that you're nice. Basically everything I know about you." He's still not looking at me in the eye, his hands turning over the keys.

"Here, let me." I take the keys from him, and the skeleton key breaks off easily, an old leaf in my hand.

"Uh, you can keep the mattress," he says, "and the dresser."

"That's so thoughtful," I say, the same way I said I was happy for him and his girlfriend.

"Rent's tomorrow," he says. "You just leave it in the mailbox downstairs. It's month to month; I think I said that. There's a house meeting later tonight, around six. You . . . wanna get dinner or anything?"

"Nope, I'm pretty full." I don't look him in the eye. I'm actually starving from the bus ride, but I'm trying to make a point. I chuck my underwear and socks into the seafoam dresser. Some blood-stained underwear hits the floor.

"We're in Somerville, so you just have to hop on the Orange Line if you ever want to come see us." Arnold looks around the room, sniffling again.

"Caroline would love to spend time with you." His hands are practically vibrating. He looks down at them and then shoves them under his armpits. He clears his throat.

He rubs his thumbs against his arms. "So, I'll see you when I see you?" He really looks so hollowed out. The skin around his eyes is veiny and purple.

"Yeah." I try to push my resentment out of my mind that, if I'm being honest with myself, is probably reserved for Jo. My old friend holds his arms out to me, two withering, familiar branches.

"Thanks for the ride." He's so skinny beneath me. I feel worried.

"Anytime." He breaks from me, and his eyes fix on something behind me again.

"What the fuck are you looking at?"

"What?"

"You keep staring out into space or staring at something. What's your deal?"

"Sorry. It's my ADHD or whatever."

"Go eat something," I say. "You're freaking me out."

"I know." He chuckles. "Caroline's waiting for me. So." He bows away through the door like some kind of waiter. I take a linty fitted sheet from my suitcase and stretch it over the stained mattress, then cover it with a blue quilt with a yellow moon stitched on the front. My dad made it for me when I was a kid. He was surprisingly domestic for a construction worker. He cried at movies. He made pies. I sit on Arnold's old mattress and cross my feet. I shiver and pull out a sweater. I try not to feel afraid, because I don't know what I should feel afraid of.

We met at a show; where else do you meet people? I'd just moved to New York and was saying yes to everything, because that was what I was told to do as an artist. Say yes until you make it and are privileged enough to finally refuse. She performed before I did, kneeling on the floor of a small apartment in Bushwick with her guitar and her pedal, making her voice push in and out of itself, saying something that sounded like "I'll eat us up" over and over again. She made me nervous, and I was nervous, anyway, invited there by a friend of a friend who hadn't even shown up, who'd just needed to fill the bill. I got up there and sang my songs about my dead dad. I was a sentimental little songwriter using the same four chords, strumming with my open thumb. I saw someone out of the corner of my eye check his phone. But Jo was making audible noises the entire time, laughing at some points even, practically moaning. She came up to me afterward with a wet face and red eyes. "I'm so starstruck by you," she said. It was irony cut open, bleeding into sincerity. We sat in a corner just talking, eventually holding hands, the rest of the party having meaningless conversations about how they should do this again. We went back to her apartment, and then I never really left. Were we in love? Maybe, but it was a different kind of love. And I don't ever want to find it again.

I order two chicken tacos from the burrito spot next door and bring them back to my room. They stink up my new room with onions and beans. I stuff my suitcase into a closet that has a half-broken hinge. I sit down on the wooden floor in front of the vanity mirror, cross-legged. I look like a cancer patient with this short hair. There's a yellow stain I hadn't noticed on the ceiling, stretching like pizza dough. I can be gone by the spring, I think. I have to. I'm nervous about meeting the housemates. If they'll recognize me. If they'll be polite enough not to say anything, which almost feels worse. At six p.m. I make my way downstairs, passing the hole. My hand is on the flaky banister. The living room has more sculptures hanging from the ceiling like meat. There's a piano shoved next to a bricked-up fireplace. There, sitting on mismatched furniture, are my housemates.

There's a couple at the far end of a tattered teal couch, one hand on the other's chest. The boyfriend is the most beautiful person I have ever seen. He has shiny dark hair that falls below his ears, purple dye slowly fading to blond at the edges, and a deep brown face that looks like it was carved from clay. I have to look away from him. The girl attached to him is tiny and forgettable. Extraordinarily plain and white. A cream cheese kind of person. If she weren't wearing a fashionable leather jacket, she would look just like all the blurry girls on my feed, making Boomerangs at brunch. I think about the girlfriend's hand breaking off as it separates from the boyfriend's chest, the crumbs from her skin rolling around the floor like dust from marble.

Bell sits in a yellow chair that frays on the left arm, his skinny ankle moving gracefully in a circle. A girl with baby bangs who might be Puerto Rican or something is wearing the same sweater as me, knitted, diamonds, colorful, looks like Bill Cosby would've worn it. There's also another white woman, with green hair and bruises all around her arms. Next to her is an extremely poised Black man sitting with his legs crossed, looking like he hates being here. What do I say if they know who I am? I stand by the doorway, one hand on my elbow. The woman with green hair and bruises starts to talk.

"Should I go? I don't know. I feel like I always go, and then there's this weird thing about how I'm bossy."

"Go ahead," Bell says, gentle and kind. "You're not bossy." There's a little jingling sound. A tiny white dog in a diaper scoots herself into the common space, the bottom half of her aided by a pair of red wheels fastened to her hips. As she scoots, she leaves behind a soupy brown liquid. The Black man who had his legs crossed now uncrosses them, pointing his finger at the mess.

"We need to talk about that."

"That's what we're here for, Gary," the woman with green hair says.

"Every day I'm cleaning up this dog's shit, *Judy*."

"It's not *shit*."

"I don't even want to know what that means. I don't know what's up with this dog. It freaks me out! It freaks everybody out!" The dog's wheels are now stuck between two rooms, and her grimy paws move pathetically forward, drowning on land. She gives up and rests her head on the broken tile floors.

"If this is about the poop she ate off the floor the other day," Judy says, "I am certain that wasn't hers." The housemates all look at one another.

"Are you accusing one of us of shitting on the floor?" Gary asks, his hand to his chest.

"Judy is tired, isn't she?" Judy the person sits down next to, I guess, Judy the *dog* and strokes her head. Gary takes out his phone. Bell chooses his words carefully.

"I feel like maybe we should say hi to the new roomies? Would that be okay?" Everyone consents.

"This is Farah. I just met her over the hole."

"Hi," I say. I've been at the edge of the doorway, just watching. "Do you want me to get a paper towel or anything?" I point at the liquid trail on the floor.

"That's okay," Judy the person says. "Time heals all wounds." Gary gasps a little bit. Then I have a sneeze attack. Five sneezes, all in a row.

"Bless you," the girl with baby bangs says. She's the other new roommate. "What's up, everybody? I'm Polly."

"I'm Stacy!" That's the girlfriend's name.

"And I'm the boyfriend," the Boyfriend says. There's a faded Pile poster behind him on the wall. Everybody giggles. It's a joke, but then he doesn't say his name at all.

"Are there other roommates?"

"Yeah," the Boyfriend says. "But we hardly ever see them."

"I don't even know their names," Stacy says, scratching her eyebrow. "One is Mary?"

"Marcia, I think," the Boyfriend corrects.

"Whatever. It doesn't matter. You'll never see them. People go on tour a lot."

"But how many more are there?"

"Oh, I don't even know. They're in and out. Like, four? Five?"

"That sounds right," the Boyfriend says. His hands remind me of tiny wooden figurines without faces in art class, those knots that tie the limbs together.

Gary stands up. "I said what I needed to say." He makes his way up the stairs, then stops and calls down, "And can someone wash the goddamn dishes? The sink is gaining sentience." I take his seat.

"Arnold said that you're very talented," Stacy says, cocking her head at me like one of those prehistoric dinosaurs that are birds now.

"Oh yeah. Arnie is the best," I say, laughing probably too hard and picking at the wooden slats of the chair. "I'm okay." How much did Arnold tell them?

"I'm sure you're fantastic," the Boyfriend says, giving me a wink that makes my face flush. Judy grabs Judy the dog from where she got stuck in between the living room and the kitchen. Judy the dog happily licks Judy's face.

"Good night, guys," Judy says. It's only six thirty, but in the living room, it might as well be midnight. "It was really nice to meet you." Judy slides away with Judy the dog in her arms, barely making any noise as she climbs up the flaky staircase. I think I hear her crying.

Bell stands up, one slipper falling off his foot. The foot chases the slipper back. "I'm gonna head to bed, too," he says sweetly. "Nice to meet you both. There's a lot of new energy. I'm just processing a lot. So I need to be by myself." The patchouli smell fills my nose again as he leaves. Now it's just us four. The tip of my nose is freezing, and all I can think about is how I want them to like me.

"Is that the same hole from upstairs?" I ask, pointing to where I can see it in the kitchen and filling the silence.

"What hole?" Stacy tucks her feet underneath the Boyfriend's legs.

"The hole in the hallway?"

"Oh, right." Stacy runs her hand through her stringy hair and laughs like a politician. "We actually don't have to deal with the hole anymore because the two of us"—she squeezes the Boyfriend's knobby hand—"moved to the fourth floor. We get the entire upstairs to ourselves!"

"There's a fourth floor?" I ask. "I counted only three from the outside."

"What's that disease where you can't look at a lot of holes at once?" the Boyfriend asks. Nobody answers me about the amount of floors.

"Tropophobia," Polly says. "And it's not a disease. It's a fear."

"Right," he says, clapping his hands together. "I feel like I have that."

"So, what's up with the dog?" Polly asks, a shadow of gossip stepping in front of her face. Stacy and the Boyfriend look at each other. Stacy begins in a low, conspiratorial voice.

"Judy got an emotional support dog for her anxiety, and her name is also Judy. None of us can tell if she named the dog Judy or if she found a dog named Judy. And both Judys have anxiety?"

"And they're *both* taking CBD oil." The Boyfriend also speaks low. "But then, Judy the dog's hip broke somehow."

"So that's why she has a wheelchair. It's pretty sad." There's a silence, a measuring of the room, and then something clicks, and we all laugh. The Boyfriend scrunches up his eyes and lets out air slowly from his mouth, like it's being squeezed from a tube, and Polly covers her mouth and moves like a saltshaker, and I find myself pulled by it, too, the maniacal laughter I felt when I was in middle school, sitting in a circle with friends I don't even know anymore, the saliva filling my mouth and making my eyes dilate, when everything is funny but also I could cry at any second. They like me. They share gossip with me. And they don't know anything about me. And now we're sitting, the four of us, hooting and hollering like we've known one another for many, many years. Just then, a hammering sound comes from within the walls, like there are tiny little fists begging to be let out.

"What was that?" Polly says.

"Pipes," Stacy says. "It's an old house."

"Arnold said the heat doesn't work."

"Yeah," Stacy says, like I'm an idiot, "exactly."

Jo grew up in Manhattan, so she always seemed older than she was. All her friends were children of celebrity-adjacent people. She had the same coke dealer as Selena Gomez. She was mentally ill, immorally privileged, and immeasurably talented. That's the worst part out of all this. All that bullshit and she was still so fucking good at music. She could hear a song and play it by ear within five minutes. She was a nerd about music theory, but then would say it didn't really matter, but then would implement it in all our songs. One day, she saw my beat-up baby blue Fender I had spent the summer of senior year saving up for getting sexually harassed working at a diner, and she winced. "Let's fix this. You need to be playing something real," she said. "Because you're the real deal." She took me to a Guitar Center. I touched a bright green Les Paul. She got on the phone with her dad and started yelling at him.

"I need you to wire me twenty-five hundred dollars right now. It's an emergency." I waved my hands in front of her face. This was humiliating. I thought of how my parents never accepted money from other people. I couldn't bear someone spending this much money on me. She shook her head at me, almost annoyed.

"Can you do it? Now. Thanks, Brian." She swiped her card. I sold the guitar on Craigslist to some dude in Ridgewood right before I came here so I could have money for rent.

I rip a new toothbrush out of its plastic casing and feel depressed holding it. I walk with it in my fist, like I'm holding a lonely candle or a knife to kill myself with, to the bathroom downstairs and flick on the light. There's a large painting of a panther with yellow eyes, surrounded by trees, sitting on top of the radiator. It's kind of a shitty painting. The trees behind the panther are a sloppy brown and look like little pieces of jerky shooting out from the ground. The moon's a circle made with a protractor—I can see the pencil etching behind it. But there's something about the way the light hits the panther's jaw and over the curve of the panther's snout, something about the bright school-bus eyes, that makes me brush my teeth harder. I want to get out of there as fast as possible. It's stupid. I'm projecting my worries onto inanimate objects. It's dumb. I'm just seeing things. Still, I brush my teeth so hard and so quick that my gums start to bleed.

I spit the blood out into the sink and turn the faucet on. It clogs, and the water's murky with my gum blood. I open the bathroom mirror to tuck away my toothbrush, but it's slimy from the decaying spit of my housemates and old pill bottles. I shut the mirror slowly, thinking about classic movie jump scares. But nobody's there. Just me and my bad haircut. I need a hat or something. My eyes look swollen. I turn off the light and bolt upstairs and through the hallway, where my socks make me slip and fall. I feel the toothbrush escape my grip and drop into the hole. Fuck. I crouch and shove my hand in there like I'm fisting it and move my fingers around. I feel nothing but cold air. I make my way downstairs again, the dust accumulating on my socks, passing the bathroom and the glaring panther again. I feel like I can see its eyes even with the lights off. In the kitchen I move around chairs, saltshakers, random scarves and jackets, bottles of gin, and scrunchies, searching for my toothbrush. I step onto the seat of a wooden chair and reach into the hole with my hands. Nothing but air.

WERE YOU IN MY ROOM LAST NIGHT?

Fame happened the way most love stories do: all at once, sweeping us up before we were even ready. We wrote "Fade" in five minutes. I always thought it was annoying when people said they wrote songs in five minutes, but now I know they were just on a lot of Adderall. The drumbeat was simple, the guitar chords, too. A troll on one of our videos in the future would say that this was just like the Beatles, and he wouldn't mean that in a good way. A child could have done it, and that was why it was so popular. It was a beat you felt in your heart and in the nervous shaking of your knee. "This is the way I was made," we sang. "This is a love that will fade." She had a brief tantrum—she was always really impatient—trying to figure out how to upload it to Bandcamp, and then we shut off our screens for forty-eight hours. A popular artist found it and shared it, and then suddenly our inbox was full of people asking us if we wanted to be on a bill. The next week, we played a sold-out show at Pianos. We didn't even have any merch.

They asked us if we were queer, and we always answered yes. They asked us if we were dating, and we never answered. They loved that I was a queer woman of color being loud about my sexuality, which I had never truly explored. There were accounts dedicated to us, holding hands or whispering into each other's ears. They asked Jo if she was gender nonconforming, and she said yes, since she'd been seven. When I asked her if she wanted me to change her pronouns, she said of course not; that was just for publicity. When Jo asked me to change the pronouns in one of my songs to "she," I told her that the song was about my dad. She said nobody had to know that. "She's Gone" was our hit. Everyone thought it was about a girl I loved who went away. It was the song people took out their phones for. It was the top played song on Spotify before they took us down. We performed in our underwear, pubes out. We left glitter everywhere we went.

I secure a job at a thrift store on Washington Street where I sift through the donations: boxes of old photographs, maternity jeans, mirrors. If they're sellable, I tag them, place them on hangers, and sort them through the store. It's cool to be part of the process of bringing unwanted things a new life, a new home. My dad used to love thrift stores for all their quilt-making materials. He and my mom would fight about the junk he'd keep in the house. He would say that unfinished projects were just guaranteed days of the future. We donated all his fabrics to Goodwill a few weeks after he died.

A yellow table comes in during one of my shifts. It feels welcoming to me in a way. I hear it, actually. I hear it saying, *Take me with you. I'm made for you.* I walk home carrying it, using my core so I don't hurt my back, and I think that if anyone were about to pick me up, I would say, *The landmark you should look out for is a girl holding a yellow table*, and that would be the only thing I ever was. I reach Gray Haus and set the table down on the porch, digging for my keys. I hear the stairs on the porch creaking. It's Polly, wearing bleached overalls and a pink T-shirt with a blue heart.

"Do you need any help?" Polly and I have matching bags under our eyes. These last few weeks, I've felt as though I am sleeping too much and not enough.

"If you want." I jiggle the key through the lock, and the door flings open, as if I pushed it. Polly snatches the yellow table with ease and follows me upstairs. Polly has bruises on the bicep of her left arm, just like Judy does. They're the sort of bruises that happen if a lover squeezes you in a familiar way or you run into an unfamiliar door. We walk slowly through the hallway of flaky wall skin, carefully avoiding the hole in the floor. I open the door to my bedroom, and there's Judy the dog, sitting and looking up at us with expectant, wet eyes. She's left a trail of shit juice on the floor.

"That dog is so fucked up," Polly says, flinging herself to sit on the mattress. I still don't have a bed frame. I scratch at my eyes.

"Yeah, I feel kind of bad for her." I scoop Judy up and place her outside.

"Was this already here?" Polly asks, patting the comforter with the moon on it.

"Uh-huh." I push the table next to the bed.

"Aren't you scared of bedbugs or anything?"

"It was my friend Arnold's. I trust him. And, you know, that's kind of a moot point living here."

"So true," Polly says. I walk to the bathroom and grab fistfuls of toilet paper. I see the panther, ignore it. I walk back to my room, where I grit my teeth and wipe Judy the dog's juices away. I toss the toilet paper into the pink plastic trash can I got from the thrift store. I agonize over having to throw it out.

"Anyone hot at the thrift store?" Polly asks, lounging on my bed like she's part of an expensive painting. I lie down next to her and place my hands on my stomach. We stare at the ceiling and the yellow stain stretching across it. I sniffle.

"Mostly just old ladies."

"Old ladies can be hotties."

"I kinda can't *wait* to be an old lady."

"Me too. We can be scary old ladies together. We can eat up the neighborhood kids."

"The ones we don't eat, we can train to be scary old ladies."

"We also don't have to eat any children. That's completely optional."

"Right, absolutely optional, but every scary old lady has a right to what she consumes."

"Oh yeah, one *thousand* percent."

We laugh together easily, and I think of Jo, how we would wheeze together, not being able to breathe from laughing so hard.

"Hey, were you in my room last night?" Polly asks me conspiratorially, like we are both the same kind of pervert.

"I don't think so," I say. "Fuck."

"What?" In the bed here with Polly, I feel a comradery, a sisterliness that comes from living together in a shitty situation. Maybe she won't judge me.

"I sleepwalk when I'm anxious."

"Oh, got it. It's okay! It happens. My anxiety makes me do the craziest things. I used to be kind of bald because I would pull out all my hair."

"Whoa." I imagine Polly bald.

"I know, right?" We laugh and laugh. I hear Judy the dog lugging her body across the cold hallway. There are thuds from upstairs again, bouncing steps moving from one side of the wall to the other.

"Do we know who's fucking doing that?" I ask.

"I think it's the Boyfriend," Polly says. "He looks like a dancer. With that sexy little body." She snorts through her nose, and I put a hand over my mouth, giggling. We stop laughing and stare at the yellow stain together.

"I think the panther's a girl," I say.

"What?"

"The panther in the bathroom."

"Oh, that shit is so ugly. We should redo this entire house."

"Yeah, we should."

"We could make it so beautiful. Paint it. Really go to town cleaning the floors. Plug up that hole."

"Yeah," I say. "It could be really nice."

I was very nervous before our Spotify Live session. We were getting all these write-ups in the press. People wanted us to play, wanted to interview us about our story. I want to say it was overwhelming, but actually, it just felt good. It felt so good that I almost couldn't feel it. I was floating above it, watching myself try to feel it. Jo was nervous, too, and because of that, she got drunk. She was a drunk who got really articulate and CEO-like when sloshed. She gave me a pep talk in the bathroom. "You're a star, you were meant for this, nobody is doing it like you, nobody is doing it like us." She cupped my face in her hands. "Everybody wants you," she said.

I'M NOT A MONSTER

I wake up at 3:34 a.m. outside of Gary's room, curled into a ball. He gently shakes me awake. "Hey, you okay?" I feel like I've been drinking all night. "Yes," I say, "I'm sorry, Gary." He helps me to my feet and says, "You drunk or something?" I brush my hair back, wipe my mouth with my hand. "I was just . . ." I say. "I was trying something out." Gary narrows his eyes at me, shakes his head, mutters something about white women, and closes the door. *I'm not white*, I wanna say. I mean, my mom is, technically. But that would be unhelpful. I look the way that I look.

I have to pee very badly. I walk barefoot across the hallway and make my way down the flaky stairs. I turn on the light in the bathroom and am face-to-face with the panther. I sit on the toilet, tapping my foot up and down. It smells like old pee in here. I have blue nail polish in the shape of broccoli on my big toe, left over from New York. I can't bring myself to get rid of it. I wash my hands and fill up a cup of water. I open the door, and there is the Boyfriend. He isn't wearing a shirt. I'm staring at his nipples. They are brown and hairless like the rest of his body. He smiles in a domestic way, like I could see him over a glass of orange juice and a stack of pancakes. He is every best friend's hot older brother. He is the boy you ask stupid questions to, like *What is your middle name? What floor are we on?*

"Hey," he says.

"Hi," I say.

"Staying hydrated? That's important."

"Yup." I try to pull my shirt down. I realize I'm not wearing underwear. "Are you practicing for a performance or something?"

"No. I'm a social worker."

"Oh. So that isn't you upstairs? Dancing?"

"Must be one of the other roommates." We're standing too close to each other.

"Right," I say, switching my balance to the other foot.

"Have a good night," he says, tipping his head at me and brushing past.

"Good night."

I walk back across the chilly wooden floors, smiling to myself like a fucking loser. Were we flirting? Is it always flirting a little bit when you talk about water? When you wish somebody a "good night"? I trip over a nail, bouncing on my bare foot, yowling. My cup of water escapes my hands, but I don't hear it land. I get down on my knees and swipe, trying to find the glass. It isn't there. The hole. I get scared all of a sudden and run to bed, pulling the covers up over my nose. My throat's so dry, but now I'm too scared to do anything about it. Maybe I'll just dry up from the inside out, whatever. I hear more scraping across the floor, and then something leaping up the stairs. I can hear them so well that I can almost see them. There are two of them, I think. They're on all fours. They're leaping into each other's arms and twirling. Sometimes they're flying. They're dancing all night, I think. They're probably really in love.

The last time I sleepwalked was about a year and a half ago, on tour in Nebraska. We stayed in this hotel that gave me the creeps, because it was casino-themed but nobody was playing anything. There were little arcade games all around that were lit up throughout the night. It was the anniversary of my dad's death, so Jo bought us two bottles of champagne, and we drank them all down. I woke up on the twelfth floor, Jo pulling me off the ledge.

"What the fuck were you thinking?" she said, her eyes giant and wet. I explained to her that sometimes my mom used to find me curled up in bed next to her and my dad or outside on the porch.

"Don't do that to me," she said, clutching my arms and shaking me. "If you ever think about doing that again, just think about me, okay? I need you." She held on to me, and I felt her leg hairs graze mine. The arcade games blinked around us, like they were waiting for an answer. It never happened again. But it's not like I can control it. I don't know why it's happening now.

I get myself into a comfortable rhythm. The house gets colder and colder. My hair gets longer. Polly gives me baby bangs that match hers. I take wads of cash from the ATM across the street from the burrito place and slip them into the rusty mailbox for rent. I never meet the landlord. When the leaves turn color, I start sleeping with a beanie on. I wonder how much longer I'll do this for.

One night, I make mac and cheese from the box. Several layers of grime coat the stove. I go to grab a paper towel and then remember what Judy said about Time Healing All Wounds.

"What are you making?" Stacy asks. She's sitting at the table and yawning. No silver fillings at all.

"Mac and cheese," I say, trying not to think of the Boyfriend's nipples.

"Can I get in on that?" I'm surprised by her frankness. I haven't really seen much of Stacy in the last few weeks, and now here she is, like we shower together and excavate pimples from the other's back.

"Yeah, of course."

"Thank you sooo much. I slept all afternoon and feel like I'm in the twilight zone. I always feel like I have jet lag when I'm not working." There are two purple bruises blossoming on Stacy's arm. She sees me looking at them and places a dry palm over them. Her nose is as pink as mine.

"I must've hit something without noticing," she says. "I do that all the time. So clumsy."

"Are you making mac and cheese?" Polly's voice is high and sweet as her hand wraps around the doorframe.

"Yeah," I say, the water beginning to bubble and burst. "Do you want some?" Polly looks around the room sheepishly, then nods.

"I can bring you some croissants from the bakery next time as a trade!"

"Shut up," I say. "Don't worry about it."

I serve the gooey boxed noodles on three pink plates I find in a drawer. Then the Boyfriend is at the door, also looking around expectantly.

"Sorry," I say, my mouth pursing to keep from smiling. "I don't have enough."

"I'm vegan," he says, grinning at me like he's finally told me his name. "I can still join y'all, though?" Stacy lovingly opens her arms, and the Boyfriend blows a raspberry into Stacy's neck. He reaches up to the back of a shelf and plucks off a small bottle of whiskey.

"We celebrating?" We throw up our hands and cheer, because there's nothing to really celebrate. The Boyfriend pours handsome amounts of brown whiskey into chipped mugs.

"He has a loose wrist," Stacy says, tapping him on his knobby wrist playfully. Does the Boyfriend have bruises, too? Why don't I? It doesn't matter. Bad circulation in here. Poor diets. I shouldn't think about it.

"Just trying to relax," he says. We sip on our whiskey and make jokes. The Boyfriend tells us about his day at the frame store, and Polly tells us about the customers at the bakery. Polly imitates Judy the dog, arms out, fingers scraping against the grimy kitchen table. I almost choke on my mac and cheese from laughing. Stacy and the Boyfriend are always touching. I make eye contact with him and the hairs on my arms rise.

"So, Farah." Stacy turns to me. "Do you ever sleep?"

"Yeah," I say. "Why?"

"I meant to say"—she sips from her mug—"you sounded so beautiful last night, playing the piano."

"That wasn't me."

"Oh my God. And she's humble! Look, I recorded you." She took out her phone, and there I am, playing the piano. Why hadn't she said anything if she'd been that close to me? "I haven't heard that Coldplay song in a long time. It's so sweet." My heart's in my ears. I've never played the piano while sleepwalking.

"Oh, *playing* the *piano.* I thought you said something else." I hope I don't look too suspicious. "You know when you mishear, and then an alternate universe of everything you didn't say is happening?" Stacy looks at me like a prehistoric bird dinosaur again and laughs.

"You're so interesting," she says. And then, under the table, a hand touches my leg. It's warm, and it's sending a message. *Hi,* it's saying. *I know, right? There are all these people around us, but I wish it were just you and me.* It could be Polly's hand or the Boyfriend's or even Stacy's. I don't dare touch it. I want to live in the moment between imagining it's there and discovering it. *I'm flirting with each of them,* I realize. I feel it in the way my back is straighter, lifting my breasts under my T-shirt into the air; in the way my lips are slightly pursed; and how I'm responding to their jokes with a slight air of annoyance, like we're children on a play-ground, kissing one another and running away. There's a knock on the doorframe. Judy. Human Judy. Her face is the last fruit at the bottom of a bowl, the butt of a loaf of bread, somebody clapping loudly in our faces to shake us from our daydream. Her eyes are puffy, and there's dried snot in her nostrils. She sniffles, and the air in the kitchen that had been massaging all our shoulders shifts.

"What are you guys doing?"

"Just enjoying one another's company," the Boyfriend says. The hand moves up my leg the tiniest amount, a flower's petals opening slightly within an hour.

"Want to join us?" The hand leaves my leg. I rub the warm space left behind.

"Thank you so much, guys." Judy drags a stool into our circle. "Sorry, can you scoot a little bit?" We all move around for her. "Thank you. Sorry. I've had a really bad day."

"Tell us about it," Polly offers.

"I brought Judy on a Tinder date to the park, and I think the person thinks I'm a huge freak or on the spectrum or something."

"Well, Judy is . . . a lot," Stacy says. She is kind but not dishonest.

"Are you on the spectrum?" the Boyfriend asks, genuinely.

"I just don't understand why that's important right now." Judy starts to cry.

"Why did you bring her on the date?" I ask. Judy starts to wail. Tears are dribbling down her nose. It grosses me out. I don't cry a lot. In college, when my friends would cry about boys or not feeling like enough, I'd say, "I get it. My dad is dead," and that would always make my friends laugh, the frankness of it, the tragedy. They never saw me cry. Nobody ever does. Judy's hands are red and chapped, like she has frostbite. She still has bruises going up and down her arms. I feel left out of the bruises club. I want to be handled by whatever is handling everybody else.

"Aw, Judy, it's okay, babe. You're not alone. You have us." Stacy rubs her back in soft circles like an experienced babysitter. Polly looks over at me with disgusted eyes.

"I think I'm gonna go to bed," Polly says, getting up from her chair. She adds her dish to the pile in the sink, and the dishes clank against one another. Now the dishes are a city. I remember being treated like this in middle school, for reasons I still don't understand. Like a group of girls were a force, and the force picked one girl to be horrible to. There are reasons to be annoyed at Judy, though. I'm always staring at her green hair swirled on the shower wall, for example.

"I'm going, too," I say, leaving Stacy and the Boyfriend to comfort Judy. Polly and I walk up the stairs together. She brushes up against me like a cat.

"Was that a vibe?" Polly says, whispering.

"Was it?"

"I feel like they're so in love and, like, also kind of . . . freaks."

"Yeah."

"Judy totally ruined it."

"She's such a punisher."

I wake up in the room that is all pillows, straddling one of them. There's dirt on my feet and hands, blood leaking from my right knee. I throw the pillow across the floor. My groin pulses. I wipe my hands on my legs. The pillows look like they're breathing. I stand up fast and run up the stairs, back to my room, my dirty feet thudding against the stairs, my body naturally averting the hole, which looks a little bigger, but it could be the temperature, like Bell said, how it grows bigger with heat. But it's so cold in here. I don't want to think about it.

I only ever lied to Jo once, and it was about her cat, Mr. Lemons. I don't like cats. I don't like when people make a big deal about me not liking cats. I'm allergic to cats, and they don't like me. And I hated this cat. He seemed to know that I didn't like him either, and he would follow me around everywhere. Sometimes I would try to be nice to him, let him crawl into my lap or whatever, only to feel his claws sink into my thigh. Jo was having this little affair with a married producer from LA in his second apartment in Chinatown and had been spending all her nights there. We were still living in Bed-Stuy then. I was a little annoyed. She always ditched me for her lovers. She also always forgot to feed Mr. Lemons and clean up his shit, so sometimes I would fine little turds in the kitchen. I ended up cleaning the litter box every day and feeding the poor guy, my eyes swelling every time I did. And when I would bring it up, she would be remorseful, and I would forgive her. She would leave me alone with him, and he'd try to sleep in my bed and bite my feet.

One day, there was a delivery, and I accidentally left the door open, and Mr. Lemons got out. I walked down all of Marcus Garvey looking for that fucking cat, calling his name. I found him eventually, underneath a car. I scooped him up into his carry-away bag, sneezing like crazy. I got on the B38. A little girl and her mother sat next to me, and the little girl was so excited about Mr. Lemons. "He's a baby!" she kept saying. "Hello, baby!" She was so happy, looking at the fucking cat. "Do you want him?" I said. "I just found him on the street and was about to take him to a shelter." Her mom was on the phone, yelling about health insurance. The little girl was wide-eyed and grateful. "Really?" I said yes. I wrote down the kind of food he liked and a reminder to change the litter once a day. I got off at the next stop and kept walking. I left the window open in Jo's bedroom so it looked like Mr. Lemons had escaped from there on the fire escape. When she got back from the producer's apartment, she asked me if I had seen him. "I left my window open," she said. "I'm such a fucking idiot." She started to cry, and I comforted her. "He'll come back," I said. I listened to her call for Mr. Lemons over and over again.

———

Everybody is gone on Thanksgiving. Stacy and the Boyfriend escape to Stacy's parents' home in Baltimore. Gary has a Friends-giving in Allston. Judy takes Judy the dog back to Virginia. Bell stays in his room. Polly goes to her dad's house in Connecticut. I hear the other roommates walking around but don't feel like introducing myself. My mother texts me a photo of the small tur-key she is preparing. *New recipe from Facebook Stories, baby! How is Jo? How is NYC? I miss u!* I text back, *We don't celebrate this holiday.* Why am I being mean? My mom writes back with a heart, *When are you coming to New Hampshire?* I don't respond.

At night, I hear the dancers again. They sound acrobatic, like they're doing flips. At 3:32 a.m., I wake up to scratching at the door. I sneeze and hook my shirt over my nose for warmth. It's freezing in here. I get up to pull on a beanie and a sweater. The scratching doesn't stop. Now the door's shaking. Something is try-ing to get inside. *"Go away!"* I say, but the scratching keeps going. I grab a shoe—like that's gonna help—and turn on the light, but then the shaking-scratching stops. I leave the light on and crawl back into bed and check my phone. Arnold texted me while I was asleep. *What are you doing tomorrow? Caroline and I would like to see you. Friendsgiving, lol.*

The next afternoon, I pull on shapeless mom jeans and a men's jacket from the thrift store and leave the house. I take the Orange Line all the way to Sullivan Square and walk with arms folded to the address in Somerville. Arnold opens the door. His face is full again and well-rested.

"Hey, loser." He opens his arms, and I go into them. It's good to feel something familiar. Inside, their apartment is immaculate and intentional. There's a desk by a curtained window. There's a framed *New Yorker* cover of a woman eating ice cream. There's a black IKEA coffee table that I find ugly, but I'm still jealous of how on purpose it is. Caroline is in the kitchen, and I can smell something home-cooked and cinnamony. She comes out in an apron and baby blue Crocs. The way she smiles, I can picture her and Arnold visiting New York City, taking photos on the Brooklyn Bridge.

"Oh my gosh, Farah! Hello. I've heard so much about you. Oh my gosh, *happy Thanksgiving*." She says it with a perfect mixture of irony and sincerity, giggling after the "ing." Like, how embarrassing that we keep up this colonizer tradition, and also, how lovely it is for us to all be together. She wipes her hands on her apron and waddles over to me, gives me a big, soft, unassuming hug.

"You too," I say. I am embarrassed now at how angry I was when Arnold moved out. Of course Arnold moved out to be with this sweet woman in this sweet apartment. Just the two of them.

"It's so cozy in here," I say, taking off the men's coat that is too big for me.

"I want to hear all about your music, Farah!" Caroline says. "Arnold tells me you're very talented." Arnold looks at me, embarrassed. He has to know that that is the last thing I want to talk about. I rub my hands together.

"Can I help set the table?"

"Just relax, girl. Sit down. You want some wine?" I nod enthusiastically. I can actually feel my hands and nose in here. Arnold brings over a wineglass filled halfway. They have wineglasses. Caroline calls him into the kitchen.

"Can you help me with this? This turkey is so heavy."

"I don't know why you got such a big one; it's only gonna be the three of us."

"We'll have leftovers!"

I'm so comfortable, I could fall asleep or cry. I want to listen to them say normal, boring things about leftovers forever. Maybe I can move in here with them. Maybe I can sleep on the couch. Caroline and Arnold bring out plate after plate of food. Roasted sweet potatoes. Butternut squash. Some kind of green. I hadn't realized how hungry I've been, how much I have spent the last few months begging to be filled up. Caroline lights a few more candles and places them on the table so that our faces are bathed in warm, purchased light.

"Just adds to the illusion that we have our shit together," Caroline says, shaking her head. A black cat leaps onto the table.

"Aw, come on, Fin." Arnold lifts Fin off. Fin jumps into my lap.

"Do you like cats, Farah?"

"Not really," I say. "I'm allergic. But I'm not a monster." I lightly tap the cat's back. Fin's eyes are dilated, and he's purring really intensely.

"Arnold, you didn't tell me! I would've put him in our office."

"You guys have an office?"

"Yeah, but we have to share it," Caroline says, rolling her eyes. Caroline raises her glass. "To many more Friendsgivings." We all clink.

"Where are you living again?" Caroline asks, taking a bite out of the turkey.

"Gray Haus," I say, helping myself to some more hot squash.

"Oh," Caroline looks at Arnold, who sniffs. "Really?" Her sunny face falls.

"It would've been nice to have Arnold there." I happily crunch on the peanuts that are tossed into the rice. "But he seems really happy here. And healthy. You look good, dude!" Arnold looks up at Caroline, who is now frowning, fork in midair.

"Arnold told me you were moving to a studio somewhere in Jamaica Plain."

"Ha, well, I'm definitely not doing that."

"I meant that eventually she'll live somewhere alone." Arnold slurps wine that leaves red dribble on his chin. "No one stays in that house forever. It's a super transitional space." I swallow and wonder why they're being so fucking judgmental. All couples are kind of weird. I can tell they're arguing about something silently. There are pieces of resentment peeking out between their words. Yeah, I don't want this. This whole comfortable-apartment thing, this comfortable relationship— it's all an illusion. What they both secretly want is to be shivering with excitement, alone in a bed that's just their own, a sea of potential partners dancing across their imagination on the ceiling while they fall asleep.

"I mean, I'll save up and go somewhere better," I say. "But it's good for now."

"You should get out of there as soon as you can," Caroline says, penetrating dark meat with a fork. Arnold gulps down some of his water. "Arnold, are you gonna tell her?"

"Tell me what?" I say.

"That stuff had nothing to do with the house," Arnold says, pointing his fork at himself. "That was with me."

"There's really bad mold in there," Caroline says. "It was making him hallucinate."

"Caroline, it's fine."

"I hated sleeping there," Caroline says, her voice getting higher. "I'd have nightmares all night."

"What did you see when you hallucinated?"

"You're fine." Arnold cleared his throat. "It was literally just me. I had a weird mushroom trip with, um, what's his name? Bell? It fucked me up. Don't worry about it."

"I just think you should get out of there as soon as you can," Caroline says, her eyes all sweet and concerned. Caroline looks over at Arnold, who wipes the wine from his chin and sniffs.

"Well, some of us don't have anywhere to go," I say, gripping my fork.

"I didn't mean it like that," Caroline says. "And I know how much you've been through. The stuff that happened in New York."

Fuck Caroline. She doesn't know me. I hate her right now. I hate both of them. The anger's hot inside me. I feel my eyes glowing.

"I really love what the two of you have," I say, scooping up the butternut squash and thrusting it onto my plate. It makes a noise, and Caroline jumps. "You just do the same thing every day." I smile at both of them. "All you have is each other." Caroline tucks her hair behind her ear. Arnold sniffs again. Caroline tries to talk to me about movies for the rest of dinner, mockumentary TV shows she can't stop bingeing. All I can hear is the cat pawing at the door.

When I go to say goodbye, Arnold hugs me very hard. "I'm sorry," he says. "I'm really sorry."

"Don't be sorry," I say, suddenly feeling bad. What's wrong with me? What's inside me that is so nasty? "I was being rude. The food was delicious. I'm a mess. I know." Arnold looks at me and parts his lips slightly. He hugs me again.

"Thank you so much," he says. "Goodbye."

On Christmas Eve, Polly and Stacy and the Boyfriend are all home. We sit in the common space, drinking wine out of mugs with the handles broken off, watching *Love Actually* on the Boyfriend's projector. All of us are wearing sweaters and hats because it is, once again, freezing. Just as the secretary is getting called fat even though she isn't really fat, the projector shuts off. The

Boyfriend leaps up, trying to tinker with it. It comes back on, but this time it's *The Crown*. Queen Elizabeth is in Africa, unaware that her father is about to die.

"What the hell?" The Boyfriend presses something on the projector.

"This show is so problematic," Stacy says. "Why is she in Africa?"

"Because England pillaged a lot of Africa," I say, calmly.

"Oh, sorry," Stacy says. "I didn't know that." The Boyfriend cues up *Love Actually* again, and we have a good solid five minutes of watching it before it turns back to *The Crown*. Elizabeth is writing letters to her dead father.

"I don't want to watch this," I say, setting down my mug of wine with a horse on it.

"None of us do," The Boyfriend says, a little impatient, as if we have known each other for a very long time and can be impatient with each other.

"We could all just sit and talk to one another," Stacy suggests. "I mean, why are we watching this movie, anyway? Nobody actually likes it, right?" So the Boyfriend shuts off the projector and turns on the lights. I sit cross-legged and tuck my hands underneath my butt. Stacy cocks her head at me.

"Farah, where are you from?"

"Stacy," the Boyfriend says, "you know she's Latinks."

"That's okay," I say. "My Dad was from Colombia. My mom is El Salvadorian. But her great-great-grandparents were German."

"So you're biracial, technically?" Stacy cocks her head to the other side.

"I don't know. I'm half orphan, definitely." The Boyfriend glances at me and chuckles.

"Well, I'm really sorry about that," Stacy says. "That must've been horrific."

"Yeah," I say, cocking my head and mirroring her.

"And anyway, that's not even what I *meant*. I meant, are you from here? Like, did you grow up in New York?"

"No," I say. "I'm from here. Dunkies and the Celtics. CITGO signs. That's my culture."

"So why did you move back?" Stacy has her hand on the Boyfriend's thigh. Is she upset with me? I swallow.

"I just needed to get out of New York." I hope I don't have to say more. Stacy uncrosses her legs.

"Okay, I mean, we know who you are, Farah."

"You do?"

"Of course we do; we don't live under a rock. 'She's Gone' is, like, the queer anthem of this decade," she says, her hand gripping her boyfriend's thigh.

"Oh, nice," I say, like she's telling me about somebody else. "That song is pretty special." My heart's hammering in my chest. "So, um." I sip some wine. "I guess you want to know what happened?"

"Don't feel pressured to share," the Boyfriend says. He is annoyed with Stacy. I can tell. He's on my side.

"Totally," Stacy says. "No, you don't have to share anything at all. I just feel like . . . I just feel like it's weird not to bring it up. And we've all already gotten so close." Polly's shifting in her seat. Everyone's kind of mad at Stacy for me right now. Or maybe everybody doesn't want to know what happened because it would change their opinion of me.

"No, I can share," I say. "I don't care." They all look at me, ready for me to put on a show. Maybe it's time. They're my friends, anyway. They won't be mad. "Basically, Jo was always, like, um, she was always flirtatious."

"Doesn't Jo use they/them pronouns?"

"That's really polite of you," I say. "But she didn't really." Polly lets out a dramatic gasp. "Okay," she says, "*tea!*" I smile. Am I enjoying this? Maybe this is kind of a funny story. I continue.

"So, there was this fan who really liked us. He would DM us sometimes and like, bring us cookies. It was sweet." They all lean in. "And Jo would talk to him mostly. I didn't really like interacting with fans. I'm kind of bad at putting on a face. He came to one of our shows, and Jo put him on the list. She asked me if I thought he was cute, and I was like, 'Sure, I don't know.' Jo and I never really shared a type. After the show, she brought him to the hotel room, and I was like, 'Jo, I'm tired. I'm just gonna go to sleep.' And before that, I noticed that he was really fucked up. Just, like, not really there. But Jo wasn't really either. I fell asleep on the couch, and then when I woke up, he was there with her, naked in bed. I went to take a shower, then I went down to the lobby to get coffee. Then I waited in the van."

"So that's why you got canceled?" Stacy blurts out. I was waiting for that.

"No." I glare at her. I'm not afraid of her. And I see her get smaller. I feel a little powerful.

"We were recording a song a month later when the fan made the call-out post. I asked Jo what happened and she said she didn't remember. That they had both just blacked out. I believed her." The pipe sounds from inside the walls start again, the thumping, the tiny fists begging to be let out.

"And it only took hours. It was insane. People were in my DMs calling me a rapist. Telling me to kill myself. Jo's dad is super rich, so he ended up paying the guy to stop talking, but by then, it was too late. And we were about to release the greatest album ever. Like, ever. I put everything into it. And now there's just nothing." Is it happening? I start to cry. "It's all gone. And, you know, I know I messed up. But I trusted her!" The tears don't stop. I am choking on my sobs, practically drowning myself. This never happens. I'm blubbering. I'm showing them the worst part of me. Why? So I can control the fucking narrative? Polly scootches next to me and wraps her arms around me.

"Thank you for sharing that," she says. "I'm sorry if you felt pressured to." Polly throws an ugly look at Stacy. Polly really is my friend.

"I'm sorry that happened," Stacy says. "I can't imagine what you're feeling." All she has to do in this world is not be able to imagine the worst thing to happen to someone and tell them that.

"It must've been hard for you," the Boyfriend adds, and his eyes are gentle, and they are for me. The pipe sounds stop, and then, briefly, the lights flicker.

"This place is so ghetto," the Boyfriend says, trying to break the tension.

"Baby, you can't say that." Stacy looks at him like he's her son or something.

"Really?" He purses his lips. "'Cause I feel like *I* can." Stacy blushes. Polly sits in between my legs on the ground, and I find myself stroking her hair.

"Does anyone else have trouble sleeping sometimes?" Polly's eyes slowly close.

"A little bit," Stacy says, absently staring at the ceiling and then resting her head on the Boyfriend's shoulder.

"I feel like I keep bumping into stuff in my sleep," Polly says. "I keep waking up with bruises. Maybe I have leukemia."

"Maybe we *all* have leukemia," the Boyfriend suggests.

"That's stupid," I say, and I think I see Stacy eyes dilate.

"Ow!" Polly says, grabbing her hair. "Your nails." I didn't realize I was scratching her.

"Maybe this place is haunted," Polly says, laughing to herself, embarrassed, a stupid suggestion, a small offering of a smashed

banana in a Ziploc bag after someone said that they were
starving.

"I think that sometimes energy stays in places." Stacy takes
another sip from her wine. "Like, a person washing their dishes in
the kitchen sink. Places where you go over and over. Part of you
stays there. I think the kitchen sink is the most haunted place in
America."

"Stacy is a big expert on this, apparently." The Boyfriend is
teasing. They kiss. There's a small bruise on Polly's neck. Or is that
a birthmark?

"Nah," the Boyfriend says, "this place is just busted." Polly and
I laugh. Judy the dog scrapes her way into the common room,
once again getting stuck in the doorway. "I thought they were still
in Virginia."

"Did she fucking *leave the dog here*?" Polly sits up, rubbing
her eyes.

"If anything is haunting the house, it's that fucking thing," I
say. But nobody laughs at Judy. I feel the sting and the cruelty of
what I said when the Boyfriend gives into the dog's squeals and
lifts her up into the room so that she can join us.

"Merry Christmas, Judy!" She gives us a wet, little bark. We all
cheer. I feel like I'm clapping too loudly.

Bringing up Jo gives me the courage to open my email for the first
time in months. More messages telling me to kill myself, more

people doing think pieces on fake queers in the music scene, a message from my manager asking if I would want to song write under a different name for an influencer. And an email from Jo, from a month ago.

> Hi,
>
> I know you might hate me right now, and I would, too. I miss you. I'm in Spain right now. I've been sober for two months. Is it psychotic to ask you to come visit me? I can pay for the tickets. I'm so sorry about everything that went down. That guy is so fucked up. Anytime you need me, I'm here. Seriously.
>
> I love you,
>
> Jo

I can't help it. It feels like the sun coming out.

OLD GIRL

Somehow it's already the New Year. A childish part of me wants to hold the entire year in my heart, reflect on it, write about it in a journal, then let it go, but what's the point? The year was bad. I lost a lot. The ball drops. Our wishes and resolutions: Judy wants to fall in love. Gary wants to be hot. Polly wants to shave her head. Stacy and the Boyfriend say something about buying baby chickens. I change the subject. Bell toasts with his mug of whiskey. Judy gives Judy the dog a wet slobber on the mouth. Gary licks his boyfriend. Polly and I peck each other on the mouth and laugh while Stacy and the Boyfriend make out. The other roommates are here but drifting in and out of the room. One of them introduces themself to me, but they say their name too quietly. Sophie or something. Alcohol makes my bladder swell, and I wiggle out of my sparkly New Year's romper and tap my foot against the cold tile floors. I make myself look at the panther, just for one second. If I turn, I will see the panther, and the panther will just be a painting, not a real live gigantic cat. I turn my head slowly to the left. It hurts, almost, how slowly I am moving my head. I'm pretty wasted. I face the panther's yellow eyes and see one small flash of black, a lid quickly closing and then flicking back open. I shoot my arms into the tight sleeves of my romper, leaving the bathroom with my zipper open and without washing my hands. I breathe through my mouth because my nose is all stuffed. I think of the mold Caroline was talking about, sailing through the air and finding a home inside my nostrils. When I go to sleep, the dancers upstairs are doing a two-step. I can see the ceiling shake.

Jo sends another email, on my dad's birthday.

Hey, babe,

I know this day is hard for you. I wanted to tell you that you are

1) a badass bitch,

2) a fucking talented cunt with an amazing voice that people would kill for,

3) truly admirable and strong.

I love you. Please think about what I said about Spain.

Jo

I hate the way she can talk like this, with sincerity that's so bleeding and flowery that it cancels itself out. It feels like she's making fun of me. I shut my laptop.

I keep waking up in different parts of the house: the pillow room again, sitting by the piano—sometimes I'm just outside. I rarely eat, but I'm so hungry. My jeans are loose around my waist, and I hate that I like that. At night, there's somebody by my bed. It looks like Polly, but it could be Jo, too. I can't really see her face. "You're so good," she says to me. "And you're so smart and funny. You're so talented." Her hair tickles my face. Is she going to kiss me? "You're a good friend. You are a good daughter. Hi. Hi. Hi. Hi." She keeps saying, "Hi." I need to get out of here.

Gary's going to have a Valentine's Day party. There will be music, comedy, poetry. It's a fundraiser, but Gary keeps avoiding saying who it's for, which probably means it's so he can pay rent.

I volunteer to make banana bread because it is the only thing I can make. My dad's recipe. The secret is adding a spoonful of sour cream. I think about saying this later, that it's my dad's recipe, the secret sour cream, and that I made it for a friend once when she was feeling bad and how I won't say who the friend is. Polly's making an appetizer. Something with cheese and chips. Stacy and the Boyfriend are gonna make a special cocktail together and pour them evenly into cups. Bell will help with sound. Judy asks if she can read a poem or two. Gary tells her she has exactly three minutes maximum. Judy cries about that and says that time limits really hurt her confidence problems because she has Rejection Sensitive Dysphoria. Gary says, "You have what?"

I sort incoming clothes in a trance. I give customers the keys to the dressing rooms with a sleepy smile. I sort hats by size even though they are all in a bin you can reach into. I can close my eyes and reach and reach and pick out the one that is meant for me. I can be anybody I want in any hat.

"I saw her walking down the street with a yellow table."

"I thought she was in New York?"

"Guess she moved *back*." My stomach sinks. I hang on to the belts. I hide behind the rack of jackets for women.

"Does seeing her trigger you?"

"I'll be fine. I'm honestly praying for her. People who support that kind of abuse are seriously fucked."

"Are you going to that party later?"

"I think so."

I walk to the employee bathroom and try to control my breaths. I grip the cold basin of the sink I just bleached. I sit on the toilet. I brush my face with the back of my hand. The only way I can get through this party is to get drunk. I forget about the banana bread and instead bring home three bottles of vodka and some cheap cranberry and mango juice. When I get home, the bottles stretching against the skin of the plastic bag, I see Stacy, all puffy-faced and crying, on her way out.

"Are you okay?" I try to sound genuine.

"My dad . . . I have to go. I'm sorry I can't help out with the party," she says, brushing past me and walking furiously away from the house. I don't think too much more of this. The social obligation of asking if someone is okay was completed.

I find a giant blue ceramic bowl in the cupboard and blow dust off it. I pour the drinks all in together. I write *LOVE PUNCH* on a linty name tag and press it down onto the table. I take a sip. I slip on a skimpy red dress from work and stick my hair into two space buns. I go downstairs with my mug of Love Punch and ask Gary, who is hanging up streamers in the common area, if he needs help.

"You can clean the windows, if you want."

"Are there paper towels now?"

"You can get paper towels, if you want."

"Okay," I say. I'm not gonna go buy paper towels.

Bell is in the pillow room, lying down and reading a book with his feet crossed. He has his slippers on still.

"Are you excited for the party?"

"Of course. I love parties." Bell sounds like he's reading a script. His sleeves shift downward as he holds the book over his face. Bruises on his wrists.

"Where did you get those?" I ask, kind of aggressively. I'm tipsy from the Love Punch.

"You don't remember?" Bell says, moving his feet behind him so it looks like he's keeping eggs warm.

"No," I say, "I don't."

"Hmm," Bell says, looking at his arms like they don't belong to him. He hugs a pillow, wraps his legs around it. "It doesn't really matter," he says. "Memories change." I leave him because I'm done with his hippy bullshit. I don't even know what he does all day. It's like he never leaves the house. The toilet's cold on my ass. No, the panther isn't winking at me. It definitely isn't. It has two very still yellow eyes. My eyes water. I need to drink more.

"Nobody's coming to my party!" Gary says, dramatically, only fifteen minutes after the time he told people to come. He scoops a cup into the Love Punch. "What did you put in this, Farah? Antidepressants?" A person arrives. "Good to see you, Arti." Then another person. "Hey, how's it been?" Then people with other people. "Hey, I'm Danialie's friend. I've heard a lot about you." "How do you know all these people?" I ask Gary. He looks at me funny. "They all live here. Haven't you met them?" The floorboards look like beef jerky. Bell's by a window, curled up. I see a curtain of dirty blond hair in the kitchen, sipping on whiskey. Jo? She turns around. Not Jo, but almost Jo. Ghosts who are alive. People in the kitchen. People in both common areas. People kissing in the pillow room. People drinking by the staircase. The energy stays, just like Stacy said. The energy stays. I text Arnold on my flip phone, swaying as I punch in the letters.

On a scale of 1—10, do u think Gray Haus is haunted?

My phone buzzes.

lmao
maybe.

I'm buzzing, electric all over. I'm wind, slipping through the people in the crowd. I find the Boyfriend by the piano. The Boyfriend's wearing a stupid beret.

"Nice hat you have there, old lad," I say, unsure where this accent has come from. I say "hat" like "het." I'm a queen about to go watch a horse race. He tips the het.

"Thank ya, doll. I got it at the market, see?" He's playing along. In the same exact accent. It is a game. It's a bit. Polly taps me on the shoulder.

"Better save me a seat at that piano, young lady," Polly says, squeezing the Boyfriend's shoulder.

"My, my, this is quite a party!"

"It *is*, isn't? Haven't seen one quite like this since, well, a very, very long time." We are rolling our *r*'s. I want to laugh, but we're so deep in the bit. The bit's bitten us, sunk its teeth deep into our tongues.

"Now, what would ya like to hear, ladies?" The Boyfriend dances his fingers over the keyboards, and I want to take them and stick them into my mouth.

"Play me that elegant one you played the other night, when we were all discussing the clenching."

"Ah yes, the clenching. Have we been doing too much of it?"

"No, no, we're just having a little bit of fun. And there are some things you just can't let go of, see?"

"We really did a number of them, didn't we?"

Now we laugh as if we share the same breath. What are we talking about? What's clenching? I don't care. All chemistry is about being willing to play some kind of game. What if we all grew old together? Polly, the Boyfriend, and me? What if we woke up every day, in the same bed, with the same dreams? Fuck Stacy. Gary calls everybody into the common room for the poetry reading, but we don't move an inch. Judy is reading a poem about her UTI.

"What is wrong with that girl?" Polly says, walking her fingers on my shoulders.

"None of them like her," I respond, tapping two fingers to my mouth as if I were holding a long cigarette.

"Now, that isn't very nice, is it?" The Boyfriend begins playing a little tune. We sway back and forth in rhythm. He starts to sing. *"If you're one of us . . ."*

I sing harmony, sweetly and perfectly, the way I know how. *"If you're one of us, we'll give you a little kiss."*

Polly begins massaging my back, and I touch the Boyfriend's bony knee. He is smiling the entire time, under his het.

"I say, good man, do ya think you could love me?"

"I sure think I could try." And then I kiss the Boyfriend, and the Boyfriend breaks away, surprised but still smiling, teeth wet and shiny. We have all been waiting for this for a while. He kisses Polly, and then he kisses me, hot and deep on the mouth, breathing himself into us. I kiss them on their necks and squeeze their arms, and then it is all three of us, tongues colliding and mouths smashing against skin. We creep upstairs on all fours until we reach the Boyfriend and Stacy's bedroom. "I don't think you guys have ever been up here," the Boyfriend says, gesturing at the green velvet couch they have. "Stacy keeps it really nice." But I have been in here before. I know where everything is. I know where they sleep.

Polly and I pounce on the Boyfriend. I bite at his zipper, and Polly fights with me playfully, wanting to be part of the tearing. Polly takes the Boyfriend's face in her hands, and I push her away, and the Boyfriend touches my breasts. "We've been talking about opening up," he tells us as we rub ourselves against him. Is it all for him? Who are we now? It is all for us. I cover the Boyfriend's eyes as Polly lowers her fingers into his mouth. He's breathing fast. He gains control and has us both down on the bed. Polly puts a pillow over my face as the Boyfriend buries his between my legs and Polly licks my nipples, or maybe it is the Boyfriend at my nipples, and is there a third mouth, somehow, on my neck? I breathe into and suck on the pillow, bucking my hips as all the hands keep me down.

Then it's over. We are all entangled in the other. We are all one multilimbed thing. I wake up at 3:34 a.m. needing to pee. There are still people downstairs. Slurred conversations. Someone is smoking weed. I pull on my slip and quietly make my way to the bathroom that Stacy and the Boyfriend share. There is no toilet paper. I walk downstairs to the common bathroom. Gary and Bell are on the couch together, smoking weed and laughing. I make eye contact with Gary, who looks at me deeply, inhales the joint, smiles, and then looks away. In the bathroom, the panther is breathing. I can hear the rolls of a purr in the back of her throat. I flush and leave again without washing my hands. Climbing the stairs, I hear a small scraping noise. Judy the dog again, struggling. One of her wheels is stuck in the hole. I help her out of it, and the dog slowly scoots its way toward Judy's room, where the door is open.

I can hear Judy whimpering. "Please don't hurt me anymore. Please, please, please." I peek inside, but Judy is alone in her bed, talking in her sleep. I leave the lights in the hallways on and make my way to my room, stepping over the hole. It looks like a big belly button. A mouth. The wood around it like flesh. Jerky. Is it bigger?

Did I get smaller? I want to be, very badly, alone. I sleep in my bed that was once somebody else's bed and dream of running with a dead rat in my mouth. When I wake up, I have both hands around Polly's neck, and she is purple in the face, choking. I jump off the bed, my hands shaking in front of me.

"What the fuck!" Polly gasps for air. The Boyfriend has his arm in front of her, protectively.

In the dark, we are all shadows. Two shadows holding on to each other, and the other shadow, mine, barreling away in the dark on all fours.

Stacy comes back. She had received a call from a hospital that her father had had a stroke, but when she got home, her father was asleep, watching *Jeopardy!*, feet up on the table. She curls into the Boyfriend's arms and says, "I am so happy I can depend on you." I am sleeping, but I am in the room with them. "This world is so scary and weird," she says. And this is when the Boyfriend confesses, though he reconstructs the tale. He tells her I drugged the Love Punch, and suddenly they didn't feel like themselves. He tells her that they don't remember anything. That I assaulted both of them, actually, and then they woke up with my hands around their throats. Stacy's quiet. She sits up, then stands at the end of their bed with her head down and her hands shaking.

"Is that a lie?" Stacy asks, her eyes brimming with tears. They can't see me on the ceiling.

"No," the Boyfriend says. "I would never lie to you." Stacy marches down the stairs. She's making the floor shake with the pressure of her feet. She yanks the door open to my room, where I've been napping, dreaming of them.

"Wake up," Stacy says. "I want to hear it from you. I want to hear what you did."

"What?" I say, looking at the Boyfriend and Polly, who are behind her in the doorway. I have never been this tired in my life. I sit up. My stomach's growling.

"I knew we shouldn't have trusted you, but *I* believed in giving people second chances." Are they even in my room right now? Am I? I can feel the hole stretching, its nerves breaking to let something in.

"I think this house is haunted, guys," I say, like we are all back in the common area again and nothing bad has ever happened.

"How come everyone in this house has bruises on them except for you? How come it started as soon as you moved in?"

"That's not true." I yawn. "There's always gonna be bruises. I think something is here. It's like you were talking about before; it's the energy that stays."

"Fuck the energy and fuck *you*."

Polly and the Boyfriend look away from each other with their arms folded. I want to tell them that they all have to leave. All of us have to get out of here before the bruising gets even worse. But I'm exhausted. I just want to sleep. I just want to dream.

"I should call the fucking police, but luckily for you, I believe in restorative justice." Stacy's face is bright red, and her fists are curled underneath the sleeves of her leather jacket.

"Okay," I say. "Thank you."

"You need to be out of the house by tomorrow." Stacy storms out of the room. Polly and the Boyfriend look at me.

"I'm sorry, Farah," Polly says. "But I think we all know that it's best if you leave." I don't care. Didn't we all fuck one another? Or did something fuck us? We're all fucked. I giggle a little bit. There are more roommates behind them. Every roommate who lives here. Ten of them. Twenty. The Boyfriend has blond hair now—when did that happen? They look disturbed watching me laugh. I brush my face with the back of my palm.

I write Jo. I tell her that, actually, I would love to come to Spain. What's the difference between us, anyway? We should both be horrible together. She emails me back right away.

> My love. I'm so excited to see you. Nobody knows who I am here. It's perfect. We will have the best time. I just bought you a one-way to Spain from Logan Airport. Do you still have your passport? Your flight leaves tomorrow afternoon.

Relief floods me. I've been saved. I am safe. I throw all my stuff into my suitcase. The dancers are at it again upstairs. *"Shut up!"* I yell. *"Stop fucking dancing!"* I moan into my pillow. Tomorrow can't come fast enough.

I sleep and I sleep. I have dreams about riding in a car again with Arnold, then the car turns into the insides of something, and we are both swishing all around in the sea of its guts. I have dreams about Jo cutting me open and eating my organs while fingering me. I wake up suddenly, well-rested. The sun's just rising. In a few weeks, it'll be spring.

I have to pee. In five hours, I'll be on a plane, and Jo will pick me up, and we'll put all this behind us. I look at the painting, and the panther licks her paw. I flush and leave the bathroom for one last time. I'm too scared to wash my hands. I hear tiny whining. A small scrape. It's Judy the dog, stuck in the hole again. I crawl to her. She has mucus around her eyes, and her white hair is stained and damp, a towel that needs to be thrown out. "You stupid little thing," I say to her. "You poor, stupid little thing." She looks so sad with her wheels, struggling, this small animal with a brain and a heartbeat, moving her way through every single day, even though it hurts her. I go to help her up, but her wheels make her slip, and she falls inside. I hear a faint thud, a small whine.

The hole is big enough now to fit my entire body. I have to go down and get her. I must. I shift one leg in and then the other and then feel myself fall, shooting down like a swallowed pill, and, no, I don't think of my father, or the way the helmet that I had spent a summer afternoon of my childhood decorating with animal stickers had slipped from his skull, or what he was picturing right before he hit the floor, and if it were me. Instead, I'm thinking about what it takes to be the thing that fills something else, and how ready, how normal, how without wounds you have to be to do the same.

Around me is the same cold, wet darkness I've always felt when I've reached into the hole. When I land, it doesn't hurt. It's like I've landed on a mattress, but it's the floor in the kitchen. I even bounce a little bit. "Judy?" I call for her. I hear her little wheels moving across the floor. There's a window facing the backyard, but the sun is just going down instead of just coming up. A faint slime covers the room. The kitchen cabinets are shimmering with them. The floor is, too. And somewhere, there's Judy's whining. I start sneezing like crazy. I rub at my eyes. I follow the whine and find the common space covered in the shimmery slime. By the doorframe is a long black tail, flicking at me. I walk to the bathroom, and instead of a panther sleeping, it's Bell, his head cradled in his hands on his side, his feet shifting in his sleep.

"This is quite a party!" I hear, softly, in my ear. I turn around. Nobody's there. In the darkness, parts are moving, and yellow eyes are blinking. There is music. A jitterbug. Shuffling all around.

"What is this place?" I say out loud, afraid but not afraid. Something soft nuzzles my waist and legs.

"You're here!"

"She's arrived!"

They're circling around me. A dark swirl.

"He said she would be perfect for us. Oh, I wish we could thank him!"

"Let me get a look at her." There she is, making her way downstairs, the head of them all, the queen with her school-bus eyes, unblinking. She is stoic and lean, her shoulders gracefully bunching up with each step. She sits on the end of the staircase, where I once made a good friend lug up my entire life.

"What is this place?" I say again. I hear a whine somewhere, but at this point, I know the dog's fate, and if I have to think about it, I've always known mine.

"Why, this is our home, old girl," the panther says. "This is where we live."

ACKNOWLEDGMENTS

"Pool House" appeared in Audible (2020) in a different version. A line in the final paragraph is an ode to "Where Are You Going, Where Have You Been?" by Joyce Carol Oates.

"Something Loving" appeared in Cake Zine's *Tough Cookie* (2023) edition as "First Fridays." Thank you Angeline, Tanya, and Alexis for editing.

The title "But I'm Still the King" is in reference to "El Rey" by Vicente Fernandez. I do not own this song or "Fix You" by Coldplay, "Someday You'll Want to Love Me" by Brenda Lee, "Skinny Love" by Bon Iver, or "Touch the Sky" by Kanye West.

I would firstly like to thank Rachel Kim, the initial reader and cheerleader of these stories in all their iterations. You saw what I was trying to do before I was doing it. Thank you. Thank you to my editors Rola Harb and Emily Bell for giving these stories so much thought, time, and guidance. Thank you to my agent Angeline Rodriguez for sticking with me every step of the way and making me feel so supported. Thank you to the entire team at Astra: Rachael Small, Tiffany Gonzalez, Alexis Nowicki, Olivia Dontsov, and Ben Schrank. Thank you to Kaitlyn San Miguel. Thank you to Luisa Dias for designing such a spectacular cover.

I could not have finished these stories without the labor of my dear friends reading these stories on their phone and their desktops at work: I want to thank Sam Rush, Blake Harper, Olivia Gatwood, Puloma Ghosh, Chris Gonzalez, Aye Ostertag, Molly McGhee, Tatiana Johnson-Borja, and Hannah Rego for giving these stories such thorough and relentless edits. For reading, love, and friendship that sustained and inspired me, thank you Will Zhang, Sophie Abromowitz, Jamie Loftus, Ariel Martinez, Christopher Lee-Rodrigeuz, Samuel Oboe Agotar Jr., Tiffany Mallery, Justin Courtney Pierre, Oz Rodriguez, Danialie Fertile, Arti Gollapudi, Alex Desimini, Han Schneider, Don Calva, Kat Rejsek, Jonny Teklit, Claudia Morales, Ryan Carson, Jon Shaw, Christine Engels, Sylvie Flanagan, El Kempner, Sarina Romero, and Jess Rizkallah.

Thank you to Paola de la Calle for her story about a small man in a yellow shirt.

Thanks to the Brooklyn Public Library and Polly's Cafe. Thank you Gretchen Alexander for the Redhook gig and my Redhook students. Thank you to my Center for Fiction students and my coworkers at the Center for Fiction café. Thank you also to the booksellers and the People Upstairs.

Thank you to my mother for protecting me from bad energy, my dad for telling the same stories over and over again and still being funny, my sisters for gossiping, and my grandmother for lighting candles for me. Los quiero mucho.

Thank you Frank and Jimmy who stepped over the keyboard while I was writing and typed in something better. I couldn't have done this without the parasites in my brain from your shit.

Thank you Miguel Salazar for buying me lunch when I was stressed out, reading these stories with a pen, fixing the printer (turning it on), feeding the cats, and reaffirming my belief in love. I would love to go the movies together this weekend, if you're around.

Chimera Singer

ABOUT THE AUTHOR

Melissa Lozada-Oliva is a poet, novelist, and screenwriter. She is the author of **peluda, Dreaming of You,** and **Candelaria**. Melissa's work has appeared in **Vulture, Harper's Bazaar**, BBC Mundo, **Audible, The Yale Review**, NPR, and more. She lives and teaches in New York City. She only prays on planes.